MW00417258

Marie Antoinette

David Adjmi

A SAMUEL FRENCH ACTING EDITION

FOUNDED 1830

SAMUELFRENCH.COM
SAMUELFRENCH-LONDON.CO.UK

Copyright © 2014 by David Adjmi

All Rights Reserved

Cover Artwork: Joel Zayac for the American Repertory Theater at Harvard University

MARIE ANTOINETTE is fully protected under the copyright laws of the United States of America, the British Commonwealth, including Canada, and all other countries of the Copyright Union. All rights, including professional and amateur stage productions, recitation, lecturing, public reading, motion picture, radio broadcasting, television and the rights of translation into foreign languages are strictly reserved.

ISBN 978-0-573-70262-4

www.SamuelFrench.com
www.SamuelFrench-London.co.uk

FOR PRODUCTION ENQUIRIES

UNITED STATES AND CANADA
Info@SamuelFrench.com
1-866-598-8449

UNITED KINGDOM AND EUROPE
Plays@SamuelFrench-London.co.uk
020-7255-4302

Each title is subject to availability from Samuel French, depending upon country of performance. Please be aware that *MARIE ANTOINETTE* may not be licensed by Samuel French in your territory. Professional and amateur producers should contact the nearest Samuel French office or licensing partner to verify availability.

CAUTION: Professional and amateur producers are hereby warned that *MARIE ANTOINETTE* is subject to a licensing fee. Publication of this play(s) does not imply availability for performance. Both amateurs and professionals considering a production are strongly advised to apply to Samuel French before starting rehearsals, advertising, or booking a theatre. A licensing fee must be paid whether the title(s) is presented for charity or gain and whether or not admission is charged. Professional/Stock licensing fees are quoted upon application to Samuel French.

No one shall make any changes in this title(s) for the purpose of production. No part of this book may be reproduced, stored in a retrieval system, or transmitted in any form, by any means, now known or yet to be invented, including mechanical, electronic, photocopying, recording, videotaping, or otherwise, without the prior written permission of the publisher. No one shall upload this title(s), or part of this title(s), to any social media websites.

For all enquiries regarding motion picture, television, and other media rights, please contact Samuel French.

MUSIC USE NOTE

Licensees are solely responsible for obtaining formal written permission from copyright owners to use copyrighted music in the performance of this play and are strongly cautioned to do so. If no such permission is obtained by the licensee, then the licensee must use only original music that the licensee owns and controls. Licensees are solely responsible and liable for all music clearances and shall indemnify the copyright owners of the play(s) and their licensing agent, Samuel French, against any costs, expenses, losses and liabilities arising from the use of music by licensees. Please contact the appropriate music licensing authority in your territory for the rights to any incidental music.

IMPORTANT BILLING AND CREDIT REQUIREMENTS

All producers of *MARIE ANTOINETTE must* give credit to the Author of the Play in all programs distributed in connection with performances of the Play, and in all instances in which the title of the Play appears for the purposes of advertising, publicizing or otherwise exploiting the Play and/ or a production. The name of the Author *must* appear on a separate line on which no other name appears, immediately following the title and *must* appear in size of type not less than fifty percent of the size of the title type.

In addition the following credit *must* be given in all programs and publicity information distributed in association with this piece:

MARIE ANTOINETTE was commissioned by Yale Repertory Theatre
James Bundy, Artistic Director, Victoria Nolan, Managing Director
and received its first public performance on September 1, 2012

MARIE ANTOINETTE had its New York Premiere at
Soho Rep.
Sarah Benson, Artistic Director
Cynthia Flowers, Executive Director

MARIE ANTOINETTE was developed, in part, with the assistance of the
Sundance Institute Theatre Program.

MARIE ANTOINETTE had its first public performance as a co-production by the Yale Repertory Theatre (James Bundy, Artistic Director; Victoria Nolan, Managing Director) and the American Repertory Theater (Diane Paulus, Artistic Director; Diane Borger, Producer) at the American Repertory Theater in Cambridge, Massachusetts on September 1, 2012. The performance was directed by Rebecca Taichman, with sets by Riccardo Hernandez, costumes by Gabriel Berry, lighting by Christopher Akerlind, sound by Matt Hubbs, choreography by Karole Armitage, and puppetry design by Matt Acheson. The Production Stage Manager was Amanda Spooner. The cast was as follows:

MARIE ANTOINETTE	Brooke Bloom
LOUIS XVI	Steven Rattazzi
JOSEPH/MR. SAUCE	Fred Arsenault
AXEL FERSEN	Jake Silbermann
THE DAUPHIN	Andrew Cekala
YOLANDE DE POLIGNAC/MRS. SAUCE	Hannah Cabell
THERESE DE LAMBALLE	Polly Lee
SHEEP	David Greenspan
ROYALIST	Vin Knight
MARIE'S COTERIE	Jo Lampert, Teale Sperling
GUARD	Brian Wiles

MARIE ANTOINETTE began performances at the Yale Repertory Theatre in New Haven, Connecticut on October 26, 2012. The cast was as follows:

MARIE ANTOINETTE	Marin Ireland
LOUIS XVI	Steven Rattazzi
JOSEPH/MR. SAUCE	Fred Arsenault
AXEL FERSEN	Jake Silbermann
THE DAUPHIN	Ashton Woerz
YOLANDE DE POLIGNAC/MRS. SAUCE	Hannah Cabell
THERESE DE LAMBALLE	Polly Lee
SHEEP	David Greenspan
ROYALIST	Vin Knight
MARIE'S COTERIE	Jo Lampert, Teale Sperling
GUARD	Brian Wiles

The New York premiere of *MARIE ANTOINETTE* was produced by Soho Rep. (Sarah Benson, Artistic Director:+ Cynthia Flowers, Executive Director) and John Adrian Selzer, in association with the American Repertory Theater and Yale Repertory Theatre at Soho Rep. on October 9, 2013. The performance was directed by Rebecca Taichman, with sets by Riccardo Hernandez, costumes by Anka Lupes, lighting by Stephen Strawbridge, sound by Matt Hubbs, and choreography by Sam Pinkleton. The Production Stage Manager was Amanda Spooner. The cast was as follows:

MARIE ANTOINETTE	Marin Ireland
LOUIS XVI	Steven Rattazzi
JOSEPH/MR. SAUCE	Karl Miller
AXEL FERSEN	Chris Stack
THE DAUPHIN	Aimée Laurence
YOLANDE DE POLIGNAC/MRS. SAUCE	Marsha Stephanie Blake
THERESE DE LAMBALLE/ROYALIST	Jennifer Ikeda
SHEEP	David Greenspan
REVOLUTIONARY	Will Pullen

CHARACTERS

MARIE ANTOINETTE – Queen of France
LOUIS XVI – her husband
JOSEPH – her brother
AXEL FERSEN – a family friend she's attracted to
THE DAUPHIN – her 10 year-old son
YOLANDE DE POLIGNAC – a false friend
THERESE DE LAMBALLE – a true friend
MR SAUCE – a shopkeeper (can double with **JOSEPH**)
MRS SAUCE – his wife (can double with **POLIGNAC**)
A SHEEP
ROYALIST
REVOLUTIONARY 1,2,3 – (can all be played by one man)
TWO GUARDS – (double with **REVOLUTIONARY** and **JOSEPH**)

MISE EN PLACE

Versailles, Paris & Environs
1770's – 90's

SET

A guillotine
A palace
A carriage
Trianon & L'Hameau
Tuileries & the Jardin
Tower of the Temple
Conciergerie

NOTE ON TEXT

I tend to write for the musicality of the line, not grammatical correctness.

A double slash (//) indicates either an overlap or a jump – i.e., no break between the end of one character's speech and the beginning of the following speech.

Speech in parentheses indicates either a sidetracked thought – or footnote – within a conversation, or a shift in emphasis with no transition.

When a "?" is followed by a lowercase word that means you ask the question and keep talking without taking a beat after the question mark.

Sometimes sentences will abut with no period or punctuation This means you just keep talking without taking a beat for a period a comma.

A STOP is a pause followed by either a marked shift in tone or tempo (like a cinematic jumpcut) or *no* change in tempo whatsoever – somewhat like putting a movie on pause and then pressing play. These moments in the play are less psychological than energetic. They have a kind of focused, unpredictable stillness – like Martial Arts, where there is preparedness in the silence; where a lunge or a swift kick can be delivered from seemingly out of nowhere.

Projected titles are denoted by brackets throughout the text.

"When she walks through your bedrooms carrying butcher knives you'll know the truth."

Heiner Müller
HAMLETMACHINE

ACT ONE

1.
[TITLE: 1776] MUSIC (1770-1776) DIMS TO SILENT

(They are all taking tea in a palace. They have enormous hair.)

POLIGNAC. *(pouring)*
Tea?

MARIE. (Thanks I'll have a spot) *Oh my god* I'm picking up British affectations "I'll have a spot" //

LAMBALLE. And look what's happening in the colonies //

MARIE. Boston, I *know* //

POLIGNAC. Bedlam.

MARIE. It's crazy, and all for a spot of tea.

POLIGNAC. I hate British people, I have to say;

MARIE. Lafayette writes me letters –

POLIGNAC. Milk?

MARIE. (Yes please) But nobody speaks of revolution here have you noticed?

LAMBALLE. *(opening a case) Cachou?*

MARIE. (No thanks) The people aren't happy; Or – I don't know what they are //

LAMBALLE. There's riots.

MARIE. Are there?

POLIGNAC. But there's always riots //

MARIE. Maybe they are starving. I hear things, but then I think maybe it's all a canard? Human relations are so confusing, they should be transparent and they aren't //

9

POLIGNAC. That's true //

MARIE. And anyway one hears a number of things, there's sort of a din everywhere – well in France – it's like dishes clattering and breaking everywhere you go, have you noticed?

LAMBALLE. I know,

MARIE. These rumors It hurts my head.

POLIGNAC. We have aspirin,

LAMBALLE. Have you heard of this Rousseau?

MARIE. Who's that.

LAMBALLE. I keep hearing his name, whispers, I don't know. He writes books.

POLIGNAC. We should have him to court.

MARIE. Uch intellectuals blech *(sips)* you know what I love, *mops*!

LAMBALLE. Mops? //

MARIE. Those little lapdogs with snub noses?

POLIGNAC. That baroness What's her name //

MARIE. Yes //

POLIGNAC. She has a couple //

MARIE. Yes and we have hundreds of them in a room somewhere in the palace,

LAMBALLE. You do? //

MARIE. (Well I can't ever find it) but I hear the barking Little echoes //

POLIGNAC. Cats are more dignified than dogs.

LAMBALLE. You think?

POLIGNAC. Lick the chops, swallow it down, to me it's crude.

MARIE. I don't think so,

POLIGNAC. Well, every once in a while there's an exception.

MARIE. Exceptions prove rules! That's what my governess at Schonbrunn said.

LAMBALLE. In Austria?

MARIE. Countess Brandeiss –

POLIGNAC. Do you miss Austria, Marie?

MARIE. Well I had 124 kitchens, that was pretty interesting.

POLIGNAC. And how many in Versailles?

MARIE. You know I've never seen it all – I always take a wrong turn and end up going in circles *(laughs; sips)* Vienna has the best pastries though //

POLIGNAC. Really //

MARIE. The linzer tarts omigod //

POLIGNAC. But you're so skinny.

MARIE. *(showing off)*
Yes and I dispensed with whalebone too.

POLIGNAC. You did *not.*

MARIE. It was giving me *welts*!

POLIGNAC. You're not wearing your *corset*!?

LAMBALLE. I feel sorry for the whales.

POLIGNAC. Marie you're scandalous.

MARIE. But I set the fashions //

LAMBALLE. That's true.

POLIGNAC. But it isn't seemly –

MARIE. Seemly is relative: because of me hairdos got so high they had to raise the roofs of carriages, what was *that.*

POLIGNAC. What does Louis say?

MARIE. Oh we're always in fights,

LAMBALLE. Same old? //

MARIE. I do like to disport myself I'm sorry, even buffeted by the outcries of peasants – I'm a queen I cannot simply forfeit my luxuries.

LAMBALLE. No it'd be calamitous.

MARIE. *(sighs)* And *Versailles* //

POLIGNAC. *(sympathy)* (Darling) //

MARIE. *(rapid shift)* There's all these FUCKING rules I can't TAKE IT (I – mean – I – know – I'm – acting – all – victimized –) //

POLIGNAC. *(No)* //

MARIE. But do you know what it's like having people watch you dress, undress, eat dinner *every night* Like you're some *specimen?*

POLIGNAC. It's so invasive //

MARIE. *Invasive?* they should just press me between glass *slides.*

LAMBALLE. What are you going to do?

MARIE. I told Louis I need a new palace (I'm calling it Trianon) //

POLIGNAC. You're kidding //

MARIE. I'll live there and take my entertainments as well, and I'll have my dinner *alone* thanks //

POLIGNAC. And Louis *agreed* ?! //

MARIE. (Or with friends) *what* NO (Well there was a fracas The chords in his neck got all tight but I won in the end) //

LAMBALLE. The courtiers'll be quite angry.

MARIE. *(punctuated with rage at the end)*
    Yes I expect, but it's too bad; people aren't meant to live this way it's SUFFOCATING ME.

    (a long silence)

POLIGNAC. *(damage control)* Then you did the right thing //

MARIE. (But I do have ministrations Things like that I'm not some apostate) //

LAMBALLE. No one's saying that.

MARIE. *(tiny beat)*
    You're kind. But I know people think I'm very bad.

    (long uncomfortable pause)

POLIGNAC. *(too bright)* No.

(long uncomfortable pause)

LAMBALLE. One mustn't make too much of one's reputation.

[STOP]

MARIE. What's in this one Is it apricot? //

LAMBALLE. It's very toothsome really //

POLIGNAC. I'm such a hypocrite: My kids love junk They're always after me to buy them sweets You know cakes and things But I make them eat healthy Then I gorge at parties //

MARIE. O let them eat cake //

POLIGNAC. Isn't sugar bad for their teeth?

MARIE. You think they won't sneak it? //

POLIGNAC. That's true //

MARIE. *Try the ganache* //

LAMBALLE. It's good right?

(They eat.)

MARIE. *(eating)*

In Vienna I used to just have an espresso every day in the morning for breakfast, and like a piece of chocolate and a biscuit and that was it. And nobody stood around *watching* me eat, I just ate. And I didn't have to look at my reflection all day in gilt edged mirrors I was outside, in nature, playing. The oak trees, the firs All that sunlight? The pores of my skin drank up sunlight.

(beat)

MARIE. French people don't appreciate nature.

POLIGNAC. Go to the Bois de Boulogne.

MARIE. It's not the same thing, I'm talking about *nature!* //

POLIGNAC. How is it not the same thing! //

MARIE. That's a *park*, It's man*made* – I've been to the Bois de Boulogne ok it's not what I'm talking about.

LAMBALLE. *Qu'est que c'est?*

MARIE. I don't know; I miss those shepherds in the mountains, the sound of the Danube rolling by,

POLIGNAC. *(derision in this)* You're so *Austrian.*

(beat)

MARIE. *(stung)* Is that a *bad* thing?

(eek)

POLIGNAC. I'm not saying it's a bad // thing.

MARIE. *(mustering imperiousness)* I AM Austrian.

(long uncomfortable pause)

LAMBALLE. *(buffering)* And look how flawless your French is.

(beat)

MARIE. It's all in the gullet
right here
back of the throat.

(She rolls an "R".)

See?

*(**POLIGNAC** imitates her. **MARIE** corrects her. **POLIGNAC** tries once more. Then **LAMBALLE** gives it a go)*

(They all do it.)

[STOP]

(They look at each other — see the ridiculousness of it, they burst out laughing.)

(Pageantry, flourish; a masked ball, a quadrille)

2.
[TITLE: Versailles]

(handwritten: hear barking when she opens the door)

(The place is a mess.)

(There's lots of watches and clock parts everywhere.)

(LOUIS is in pajamas, wig unkempt, playing with a clock.)

(MARIE being dressed, it is incredibly processional.)

MARIE. Clocks undone, watch springs everywhere You're like a little boy //

LOUIS. Well I never had a childhood //

MARIE. (Don't whine) //

LOUIS. I like to take things apart and see how they work //

MARIE. That can be dangerous –

LOUIS. Hobbies are fun //

MARIE. And it's a lot of broken clocks Can't you clean this?

LOUIS. No.

MARIE. This place is a mess.

LOUIS. You make messes too you know //

MARIE. *(examining the swatch of fabric)*
But I hate any mess that isn't mine, you know that What time is it (ooh I like these little striations look) //

LOUIS. Eight.

MARIE. What //

LOUIS. EIGHT //

MARIE. *(looks at a clock)* It says four.

LOUIS. I'll fix that.

MARIE. Has it ever occurred to you to *run France?*

LOUIS. Why do you have so much contempt for me?

MARIE. It's your lassitude.

LOUIS. Do you know what DAY it is?

MARIE. Thursday?

LOUIS. It's my *birthday.*

MARIE. You expect me to remember that?

LOUIS. Yes!

MARIE. I have *fifteen* brothers and sisters, I can hardly remember their *names* //

LOUIS. I'm your *husband* //

MARIE. We're great friends you and I
  Let's not mar it with facts (By the way I need some money) //

LOUIS. Marie: this heedless // extravagance

MARIE. Its not heedless *Look* at me //

LOUIS. What:

MARIE. What do you mean *what* – This dress?!

LOUIS. What's wrong with that dress?

MARIE. Are you *kidding*?
  Moths wouldn't eat it.

LOUIS. Why do you go to the trouble of speaking to me, just send me an invoice.

MARIE. In care of: //

LOUIS. *(hurt)* You're so *mean.*

MARIE. Did you sleep well //

LOUIS. *(tantrum)* NO!

MARIE. You're cranky, go play with your clocks (Too much // rouge)

LOUIS. *(Meanie)* //

MARIE. And your wig's uncombed You should // fix it

LOUIS. And it wouldn't hurt to wear a corset or stays //

MARIE. "Stays" //

LOUIS. That's what girls wear! //

MARIE. You're so quotidian.

  (beat)

LOUIS. *(returns to his clocks, quiet)* Where are you going anyway?

MARIE. See some // friends.

  (The clocks start gonging simultaneously over her response; it's a bit chaotic as he tries to silence the various clocks.)

LOUIS. "WHAT?"

MARIE. "I'M //

LOUIS. ONE SECOND.

MARIE. *(over gongs)*
WHAT THE HELL ARE YOU DOING?

LOUIS. IT'S AN EXPERIMENT AND DON'T SWEAR.

(She dismisses her retinue.)

MARIE. YOU HAVE TO GROW UP.

LOUIS. WHAT?

(He stops the gonging.)

MARIE. I SAID YOU HAVE TO –

(beat)

MARIE. *(quiet, serious)* You have to grow up.

(beat; tone shifts)

LOUIS. It was just an experiment.
I was // seeing if

MARIE. My mother bore sixteen children
I've bore none.

(beat)

LOUIS. *(adolescent shrug)* So.

MARIE. So when are you going to give me a child.

LOUIS. *(averting his gaze)*
Are you in competition with your mother?

MARIE. I am in competition with everyone.

LOUIS. Very funny –

MARIE. Don't deflect.

(beat)

LOUIS. You know about *(whispers:) the problem.*

MARIE. The people are clamoring for an heir //

LOUIS. Well I don't know what I should do.

MARIE. You spoke to the doctor.

LOUIS. SHHH //

MARIE. Well you did!

LOUIS. Maybe it'll just resolve itself!

MARIE. Its been seven *years.* There's a lot of animus towards
    me They're saying I'm barren.

LOUIS. I don't *want* to get an operation.

MARIE. Its very minor.

LOUIS. *(tiny, sad)* It's my penis.

MARIE. Will you stop acting like a baby // I'm

LOUIS. *You* get an operation See how you like it //

MARIE. *(to herself, exiting)* Oh my god Forget it.

LOUIS. I'M ORDERING YOU NOT TO SWEAR

    (She exits.)

LOUIS. *(hurt, deflated)* Where are you going?

3.

(Late night promenade, Bois de Boulogne)

(We hear fireworks in the distance, and see, sporadically, the glare.)

FERSEN. *(takes her fan)* What's this?

MARIE. *(takes it back)* Fragonard.

(She flicks it open.)

FERSEN. Ooh la la very fancy.

MARIE. Well they do call me *the butterfly queen*.

(She fans herself, does a little spin, "flutters", trips, laughs at herself, FERSEN catches her. It's suddenly tense.)

FERSEN. Watch out little butterfly or I'll catch you in my nets.

MARIE. What'll you do.

FERSEN. Pin you to the wall;

MARIE. Then I'll scream –

FERSEN. Butterflies can't scream They just beat their little impaled wings //

MARIE. And then they get pressed in a book and forgotten That's a sad end.

FERSEN. That's life.

MARIE. *(disentangling herself from him)* Nice epaulets.

FERSEN. How're things at home?

MARIE. Louis thinks you're ignoring him.

FERSEN. Doesn't he know we're having an affair.

MARIE. We're not.

(pause)

FERSEN. Aren't we?

(beat)

MARIE. No.

FERSEN. Seems a waste.

    [STOP]

MARIE. Look I'm attracted to // you:

FERSEN. And it's // mutual

MARIE. But I'm married and people talk //

FERSEN. Not that you care a whit.

MARIE. *(posture straightening) Don't* I.

    (pause)

FERSEN. That's

    that's not the impression I get.

    (beat)

MARIE. *(regal, distant)* Your impressions are mistakenly
    formed.

    (beat)

FERSEN. Are you happy?

    (pause)

MARIE. *(resisting him)* You're forgetting your station.

    (**FERSEN** *retracts, embarrassed; looks up at the fireworks;*
    awkward silence.)

FERSEN. Look.

    All the colors.

    (Fireworks; more silence)

MARIE. The night Louis and I were married

    there was a violent thunderstorm

    and they had to cancel the fireworks

    and it's been like that ever since.

    (She looks at him; beat)

FERSEN. What are you going to do?

    (pause; **MARIE** *transfixes gaze on fireworks; she's*
    desperate to stay composed.)

MARIE. I'm a little bit trapped I'm afraid.

(pause)

FERSEN. It's a lovely night.

(silence; pace slackens)

MARIE. *(a part of her that's untouched)* Ten years from now how will you remember me.

FERSEN. Like this:

MARIE. How.

FERSEN. A butterfly with opalescent wings.

(MARIE *says nothing; we hear the fireworks.)*

FERSEN. Is that bad?

MARIE. No.

FERSEN. What's the matter?

MARIE. *(gazing absently at the glare in the sky)* Nothing. *(pause)* Sometimes I feel like a game that other people play but without me. It's kind of lonely actually.

(pause)

FERSEN. You feel used?

MARIE. Is that what I mean?

FERSEN. Don't you know?

MARIE. *(being truthful)* No.

MARIE. *(after a beat)* I'm tired.

(She rises.)

Three feet of hair is a workout I must say, I get neckaches.

(She kisses him on the cheek.)

MARIE. I'll have to speak to Leonard about it //

FERSEN. Who //

MARIE. My hairdresser; maybe I'll chop it all off.

(The sounds of a horse carriage.)

MARIE. Call me.

(She disappears in the carriage.)

4.
[TITLE: 1777]

(Palace of Versailles)

JOSEPH. You are a queen by right and // by destiny

MARIE. Do you want me to cut you up a pear // or something

JOSEPH. You rule by divine *right* // and it's

MARIE. *Yes //*

JOSEPH. Not merely a right it's a // responsi*bility*

MARIE. Yes I know THAT Joseph what's this all about really //

JOSEPH. You //

MARIE. "LOUIS IS THAT YOU" (I think he's hiding in the antechamber he's very afraid of you) I'm sorry you were saying:

(an indignant pause)

MARIE. (Sorry.)

JOSEPH. Mother is very concerned //

MARIE. About: //

JOSEPH. MARIE! //

MARIE. Yes?

(beat)

JOSEPH. You are an amiable young woman //

MARIE. (thanks) //

JOSEPH. who never thinks of anything but her amusements, her dresses, her daily // pastimes

MARIE. *(temper flaring momentarily)*
THAT'S SUCH // BULLSHIT

JOSEPH. You never read //

MARIE. *(quick)* (Because I hate reading I have very poor // concentration)

JOSEPH. You never hear *anyone* talk sense for a quarter of an hour during a // whole month, never

MARIE. That's not // true

[TITLE: A SHEEP ENTERS THE ROOM]

(A SHEEP enters the room, looks at MARIE, then turns and exits. MARIE is the only one who can see it.)

JOSEPH. think anything out, and, I am *certain*: *never* give a moment's reflection to the consequences of anything you –

(He follows her gaze, nothing. She appears completely abstracted. He's staggered.)

JOSEPH. ANTOINE!!!!!

MARIE. Did you see that?

JOSEPH. *You're not listening // to me.*

MARIE. You didn't just see a sheep?

JOSEPH. I'M SPEAKING!

MARIE. *(impatient)* Well I think it's a bit weird that a *sheep* just crossed the room, I thought it warranted a footnote in the conversation.

JOSEPH. You're hopeless //

MARIE. *(taut)* Yes I'm inept at being a queen – I have bad penmanship I'm illiterate You supersede me in *all* respects Joseph //

JOSEPH. I'm //

contempt

MARIE. You're amazing and I'm shit //

JOSEPH. I'm not *saying* // that

MARIE. That's what it YES YOU ARE – and I hate being *patronized* and now // sheep are

JOSEPH. When are you going to produce an *heir*?

(pause)

MARIE. I don't know.

JOSEPH. What do you mean 'you don't // know'

MARIE. You'll have to take it up with Louis.

JOSEPH. It's been seven years

Are you barren? //

MARIE. That's none of your fucking business //

JOSEPH. It's very *much* my business.

MARIE. Is this some kind of espionage?

JOSEPH. Mother is very concerned, you're childless, you spend too much money //

MARIE. I think I've // been

JOSEPH. Your methods of ruling are heterodox to say the least //

MARIE. That has nothing to do with me, that's Louis' fault and he's crazy, he acts like he's twelve, he's INCAPABLE of making up his mind –

JOSEPH. What are you saying Antoine That mother made a bad *match*? //

MARIE. Don't be naïve. Mother doesn't make "matches" she engineers *political* alliances – and this one's turning out to be a long suck on a dry prune frankly!

JOSEPH. I won't have you speak of mother that way!

MARIE. (Oh calm down.)

JOSEPH. You have very bad manners //

MARIE. So I've heard.

  (pause; an impasse)

MARIE. *(conciliating)* How's.
  Austria – doing.

JOSEPH. Fine.

  (beat)

MARIE. You like being emperor?

JOSEPH. It's fine.

MARIE. I'll tell you I miss Schonbrunn.
  I do, Countess Brandeiss; how is she?

JOSEPH. I don't consort with Countess Brandeiss.

MARIE. I miss having a governess.
  I wonder if she thinks of me.

  (pause)

  Well if you do run into her
  send her my love. Would you?

JOSEPH. Sure.

MARIE. She was lovely, she always let me skip my homework.

(beat)

Chocolate?

JOSEPH. No thank you.

MARIE. Parisian chocolates are lovely.

(She pops one herself, chews contemplatively.)

MARIE. Do you ever think about that Joseph? Schonbrunn, when we were kids, and oh I don't know. Just. *(he isn't responsive)* I mean it sounds stupid but – being wild, and carefree, and playing in the mountains and singing songs?

JOSEPH. "Songs."

(beat)

MARIE. *(deflating)* No. You wouldn't have time for that.

JOSEPH. *(dismissive)* Uh. Not *really*.

(beat)

MARIE. *(real pain – she can't cap it here)* Well
I'm sure you think I'm being *frivolous* but
It's been hard for me.
I've had to take leave of everything Austrian
Every stitch on my back, did you know that?
And I *miss* things, I was only fourteen when I came here.

JOSEPH. Everyone makes sacrifices.

(pause)

MARIE. *(numb)* I guess.

(pause)

MARIE. I do appreciate you coming by Joseph
I know I'm considered "difficult"
and this is all for my own good //

JOSEPH. You're the queen of France.

MARIE. I know.

JOSEPH. Mother is very *concerned.*

MARIE. And I want to dispel her fears – truly –

(**LOUIS** *peeks in; gets scared*)

Louis – there he is – you can come in it's alright.

JOSEPH. *(looks around, confused)* Louis?

MARIE. You can come in, he's not going to bite you (I don't know why he's so afraid of you, I'll get him) "LOUIS"

(*She goes out into the hall. They have a row.* **LOUIS** *enters,* **MARIE** *enters behind him.* **LOUIS** *is terribly nervous, he's shaking and sweating.*)

LOUIS. Hello Joseph //

MARIE. *(fixing his unkempt wig)* (Stand up straight) //

JOSEPH. Marie and I were just talking about you.

LOUIS. Oh you were?

JOSEPH. About why you two haven't produced an heir.

LOUIS. *(feigned deafness)* I'm

I'm

I'm *sorry?*

JOSEPH. An HEIR?

(*beat*)

LOUIS. Pardon me, do you have a handkerchief? I'm very hot.

JOSEPH. Are you impotent?

LOUIS. Am I //

JOSEPH. Marie says she isn't barren, so I'm just wondering if you're impotent. I'm sorry to be so forthright, it's just that, well we feel that seven years is a sufficient amount of time to wait for an heir.

LOUIS. Yes, I see.

MARIE. (He's not // impotent)

LOUIS. *(hysterical)* IS HE TALKING TO YOU?

(**JOSEPH** *looks at him dispassionately.*)

JOSEPH. I know this must be very sensitive // for you.

LOUIS. *Tell her to stop looking at me.*

>   *(pause)*

LOUIS. The thing is
>   Joseph
>   I get very – healthy erections.

>   *(They look at him.)*

LOUIS. There's just a problem getting the
>   the "stuff" out.

>   *(They look at him.)*

JOSEPH. "Stuff."

LOUIS. The. I //

MARIE. He needs to have a minor operation //

LOUIS. *(tantrum)* IT'S NOT MINOR.

>   *(He looks at* **JOSEPH**. *Smiles anxiously.)*

JOSEPH. Is that all it is?

MARIE. He keeps putting it off.

JOSEPH. Why don't you just have it?

LOUIS. Because
>   they
>   they cut you down there.

JOSEPH. Can't you just be a brave little man?

>   *(***LOUIS*** smiles, tries not to weep.)*

MARIE. Please be reasonable.
>   Don't you want children?

>   *(***LOUIS*** weeps quietly, nods.)*

JOSEPH. Louis.

>   *(pause)*

LOUIS. I'm very embarrassed.

JOSEPH. Don't be embarrassed it's OKAY.
>   Now come with me.

LOUIS. Where are we going?

JOSEPH. Don't be frightened.

(He mouths "I'm taking him to the doctor" to **MARIE**, *she gets all excited.* **JOSEPH** *and* **LOUIS** *exit.)*

LOUIS. *(on exiting)* Have you seen my clocks? //

JOSEPH. Do you foxhunt? //

LOUIS. I've got watchsprings.

5.

(They are surveying the grounds of L'hameau, dressed as shepherdesses.)

(Fake pastoralism)

(Herds of sheep grazing; there should be something ersatz about it.)

(MARIE's enormous spires of hair are now shorn, cut tight in "l'enfant" hairstyle, as is POLIGNAC's.)

MARIE. Tilly, my page, she's so sweet, she says I walk better than any other woman //

POLIGNAC. I love Tilly! //

MARIE. And just as you'd offer a regular person a chair you'd offer me a throne!

POLIGNAC. Awww //

MARIE. Her parents were serfs //

POLIGNAC. (There's still something of that in her)

MARIE. She pays compliments very naturally //

POLIGNAC. I love nature!

MARIE. I told you!

(points)

See the cracks in the wood that's very authentic right? The first time it looked very fake I had them do it over; and we installed this fabulous farming couple from Touraine, they do all the cheese, the dairy //

POLIGNAC. It's so cozy //

MARIE. I know I love the simplicity of it, this is all I really need //

POLIGNAC. Is that a windmill? //

MARIE. *(pouring water into bowls)* All those mirrors, those gilded things, I'm done!

POLIGNAC. What's that? //

MARIE. Sevres porcelain.

POLIGNAC. I'm supposed to drink from this?

MARIE. It's more peasanty.

(They sip.)

MARIE. I used my own breasts as a mold, it adds to the fun I thought.

*(**POLIGNAC** chokes.)*

POLIGNAC. *(bright)* Oh!

MARIE. Helen of Troy did that; she's my inspiration!

POLIGNAC. I love the Odyssey.

(beat)

MARIE. *(clueless)* What's that?

POLIGNAC. By Homer?

(pause)

MARIE. *(brazen ignorance)* Who?

(double take)

POLIGNAC. *Ho*mer?

*(**MARIE** looks at her with a blank expression.)*

[STOP]

POLIGNAC. *(stymied) I love your brooch //*

MARIE. I'm doing bows now, simplicity, clean lines, nothing too ornate, metals – no big jewels – organic flowing forms //

POLIGNAC. White organdy //

MARIE. *Exactement //*

POLIGNAC. *(inhales)* And it smells lovely //

MARIE. I have the goats and sheep perfumed, I don't like rustic smells //

POLIGNAC. That's clever //

MARIE. Do you want to play roulette later I feel like gambling.

POLIGNAC. I don't have much money with me //

MARIE. *(rapt)* You SEE: THIS is what I love, you're so SIMPLE. I just want an uncomplicated life – I'm wholesome! – I feel so misunderstood.

(She feeds a goat.)

POLIGNAC. You really are.

(beat)

MARIE. *(as she feeds goat)* We can just use my money.

POLIGNAC. What.

MARIE. For roulette.

POLIGNAC. Marie I couldn't take any more from you.

MARIE. *Arrete!*

POLIGNAC. But you've already been so generous.

MARIE. That's what friends are for! You know I got Therese a job in the palace Do you want one?

POLIGNAC. Like what?

MARIE. *(coy)* Governess?

POLIGNAC. Are you *pregnant?*

MARIE. Well: Louis had an operation.

POLIGNAC. Why? Is he alright?

MARIE. I shouldn't be telling you this but he had *(stage whisper) phimosis.*

POLIGNAC. What's *phimosis?*

MARIE. This rare disease where the orifice of the prepuce contracts when the man gets an erection and then he can't retract it.

POLIGNAC. Hmm.

MARIE. So everyone's blaming me and saying I'm barren, but it's not my fault at all (you don't mind my speaking candidly do you duchess) he just had surgery so I hope that works – "hello Isabelle" //

POLIGNAC. (Who's that) //

MARIE. (Some peasant girl we installed) //

POLIGNAC. (Sweet) //

MARIE. (She picks flowers) – oh I have to be discreet I
don't want all this to get around!

POLIGNAC. I won't say a word.

MARIE. Thanks; hey, what time is it?

POLIGNAC. Quarter after one //

MARIE. Okay so at two there's a vernissage, a friend of
Watteau, Therese said she'd meet us there.

POLIGNAC. I thought you wanted to play roulette.

MARIE. Oh that's right. Ok so we'll do the vernissage from
two to three, then kibbitz, then sneak back to trianon
and play roulette.

(A **SHEEP** *has sidled up to* **MARIE**.*)*

POLIGNAC. I think that sheep likes you:

MARIE. What, oh;

SHEEP. Baaaa.

MARIE. "Nice sheep."

(She pets it.)

POLIGNAC. That sheep really likes you.

(The **SHEEP** *nuzzles* **MARIE**.*)*

MARIE. *(pretending not to be uncomfortable)*
Well this is how it is in nature, untrammeled affection,
that's just par for the course.

SHEEP. Baaaa.

POLIGNAC. Where's the dairy I feel like making myself a
cheese plate,

MARIE. Haven't you had lunch //

POLIGNAC. No //

MARIE. O you must be famished //

POLIGNAC. And maybe a glass of Bordeaux? //

MARIE. Make a left at the windmill, and then turn right,
you'll see a row of run down shacks and then there's
the dairy –

POLIGNAC. Do you want me to bring you something?

MARIE. That's fine I'll wait here:

POLIGNAC. Ok //

SHEEP. *(nuzzling* **MARIE** *neurotically)* Baaa //

MARIE. *(pets the lamb perfunctorily)* Or maybe actually a SLIVER of vacherin and some water crackers //

POLIGNAC. That sheep's really into you //

MARIE. But just a sliver I'm on a diet //

POLIGNAC. Ok.

   *(***POLIGNAC** *exits.)*

   (The **SHEEP** *looks at* **MARIE**. **MARIE** *looks back, uncomfortable. They look at each other.)*

MARIE. *(makes a face)* What what are you *looking at*?!

SHEEP. Comment allez vous?

MARIE. *(jumps)* OH MY GOD.

SHEEP. Baaa.

MARIE. Who are you?

SHEEP. A sheep.

MARIE. You're the sheep from the other day!

SHEEP. Oui.

MARIE. Do we know each other?

SHEEP. You remember me Antoine.

MARIE. Antoine That's what the Hapsburgs call me.

SHEEP. From Austria?

MARIE. *(reluctant; a beat)* I. Don't know any sheep from Austria; *(reasserting a regal stance)* And the Duchess de Polignac will be back any //

SHEEP. Pet me.

MARIE. *(thrown)* What.

SHEEP. Please pet me.

   *(***SHEEP** *bats his eyelashes.)*

MARIE. *(looks around, embarrassed)* I pet you already.

   *(***SHEEP** *bats his eyelashes.)*

   Go – graze or something –

(They look at each other. **SHEEP** *smiles at her.)*

MARIE. You're very recalcitrant

SHEEP. I like to be pet lots.

(She reluctantly pets him.)

MARIE. You're very fleecy.

SHEEP. You can shear me too.

MARIE. That'd be nice, then I'd be like a real shepherdess.

SHEEP. Baaa.

MARIE. How do you like *l'hameau?*

SHEEP. It's nice.

MARIE. Were you out grazing? Its peaceful here isn't it? Don't you think it's like Austria?

SHEEP. Marie:

MARIE. What is it Sheep?

SHEEP. I thought I should share something with you.

*(***SHEEP*** *opens his mouth.* **MARIE** *pulls out a piece of rolled parchment.)*

MARIE. Oh!

What's this. It's a poem.

SHEEP. Read it.

MARIE. Ok.

(reads)

"There once was a queen named Marie"

(beams)

Oh that's so *sweet.*

SHEEP. Baaa.

MARIE. "There once was a queen named Marie. Who'd lick her own cunt while she'd pee – "

(beat)

MARIE. *(face contorts)* Oh.

That isn't very nice.

SHEEP. Keep reading:

(She looks at the **SHEEP***. The* **SHEEP** *looks back at her innocently, shrugs.)*

MARIE. *(continues)* "They'd tell her 'your grace
You've got pee on your face'
And she'd piss herself laughing with – "

(beat)

That's disgusting Where'd you get this?

SHEEP. Sorry.

MARIE. Who's writing these things?

SHEEP. Everyone; you should be careful;

MARIE. Of what?

SHEEP. The people are very angry //

MARIE. Oh they're always angry that's not a barometer of anything.

SHEEP. They're starving, and they're overtaxed //

MARIE. That's Louis' problem, he's working on it //

SHEEP. Baaaaa.

MARIE. Anyway this obloquy can't hurt me.

(She crumples up the parchment.)

Besides I was ridiculed for my extravagances but I'm done with all that. I've given up fashion.

SHEEP. There are pamphlets circulating that say you gave blowjobs to an entire guards regiment in a single night.

[STOP]

MARIE. *(feigning control)* Well. At least they credit me with virtuosity.

SHEEP. Step carefully.

6.
[TITLE: 10 Years Later]

(Outdoors, practicing archery)

*(**MARIE** is more modestly dressed than in previous scenes.)*

MARIE. I'm having a change of heart.

LAMBALLE. About what?

MARIE. I don't know, everything.

I think things are taking a turn for the better.

I'm still keeping those Records.

LAMBALLE. Which?

MARIE. My spending's way down //

LAMBALLE. You're keeping records?

MARIE. *I told you that.*

LAMBALLE. *(flummoxed)* When?

MARIE. I cut my spending in half. I keep my receipts,

I have this little ledger and everything.

LAMBALLE. This is incredible!

MARIE. I don't know if the rest of

France thinks it's so great.

Your turn:

*(**LAMBALLE***'s turn. A short pause as she deliberates whether to speak.)*

LAMBALLE. *(forced nonchalance)* That uh. Woman… escaped prison.

MARIE. Who?

LAMBALLE. Lamotte.

MARIE. Ugh Enough with the *necklace* already!

(an uncomfortable pause)

LAMBALLE. *(demurring)* Uh. Yes well She's. She's telling everyone you're a lesbian and that you two had this… lesbian affair.

MARIE. She's been saying that for years //

LAMBALLE. But people are starting to believe // it

MARIE. How can I be both a lesbian and blowing the whole infantry at Versailles?! //

LAMBALLE. Or //

MARIE. Be *consistent.*

LAMBALLE. (Is there any more giandua?)

MARIE. (I can get you more) – "Tilly?" //

LAMBALLE. (No that's alright My // figure)

MARIE. I mean I flirt but that's healthy Lots of women flirt. *(beat)* It's in my personality.

LAMBALLE. *(demurring)* Yes.

MARIE. You think it's too much?

LAMBALLE. *(beat; gingerly)* Maybe a little prudence isn't a bad thing.

MARIE. *("fun")* I used a know a girl called prudence, British, she had *horrible* teeth –
(beat)

MARIE. *(somber)* Yes you're right.
You know me I just hate any kind of constriction.

LAMBALLE. I know //

MARIE. I feel so hemmed in //

LAMBALLE. But you are the queen.

MARIE. Yes I am that. *(beat)* You're right. I don't know why I'm feeling so defensive; I don't have anything to prove.

LAMBALLE. And then these scurrilous rumors'll be put to rout //

MARIE. Yes //

LAMBALLE. *(sanguine smile)* And the cartoons.

(**MARIE** *eats a chocolate.*)

MARIE. Yes.

(stops chewing)
What cartoons.

LAMBALLE. *(trying to make it go away)* I've *heard*
    I haven't seen // them.

MARIE. Bullshit What are they of //

LAMBALLE. I haven't seen them Marie I // swear –

MARIE. Oh *bullshit*!

LAMBALLE. One hears things.
    [STOP]

MARIE. *(panic)* What else?

LAMBALLE. *(playing dumb)* What do you mean?

MARIE. You're such a bad liar Stop it.

    (beat)

LAMBALLE. Ok.
    There's an autobiography circulating //

MARIE. By whom?

LAMBALLE. *You* supposedly and // you're

MARIE. *Me* //

LAMBALLE. Yeah and you're confessing all your "sins" //

MARIE. "Sins"?

LAMBALLE. From when you were a prostitute?

    *(**MARIE** laughs. She stops. **LAMBALLE**'s not joking. She*
    holds her head, a migraine's coming on.)

MARIE. *(quiet)*
    Why didn't anyone give me a copy of this
    did you read it?

LAMBALLE. No //

MARIE. But people have read it
    people believe // it

LAMBALLE. It strains credulity;
    most people I spoke to // about it

MARIE. *(panic) Most?* //

LAMBALLE. I //

MARIE. Who have you spoke to?

LAMBALLE. Hardly anyone –

(pause)

MARIE. *(no affect, distant)* Oh.

Ok.

Oh so that's why I haven't seen the
Polignacs, yes I see.

(pause)

LAMBALLE. A tiny stain on one's // reputation –

MARIE. *(exasperated)* TINY?

(shift to imperiousness)

I'm a *queen* Therese not a whore.
I'll have them branded and
imprisoned for life.

LAMBALLE. Is that a Good Idea do you // think

MARIE. *(temper)* No it's not a Good Idea It's an apotheosis.

LAMBALLE. Look what happened with the Necklace.

(On the word "necklace", MARIE freezes.)

LAMBALLE. Spare yourself a second humiliation.

(Pause. Slumps. She's humbled yet again.)

MARIE. I don't even know what apotheosis means.

LAMBALLE. It'll blow over;

be patient.

(beat; she takes a breath, picks up a quiver.)

MARIE. *(weakly optimistic)* I'm spending a lot less. That's
something,

Right?

LAMBALLE. It'll blow over You'll see.

(LAMBALLE shoots an arrow.)

LAMBALLE. Crap My aim's getting worse.

MARIE. Actually, it's interesting: Louis held me the other
night; He said "I'm proud of you". He's never said that
to me.

LAMBALLE. You see?

(beat)

MARIE. *(weakly)* I suppose I am proud of myself.

(drifting further and further away, lost)

But
I know there's something
else in me that wants to get out.
A little bird beating its wings against
the inside of its cage; it's funny.

(Sound of a bird flapping its wings, louder and louder.)

7.
[TITLE: June 1789]

(Palace of Versailles)

*(**MARIE** is strung out, **LOUIS** is shuffling through his various dossiers, contracts, etc, in panic. **FERSEN** looks on, attempting to downplay his concern.)*

MARIE. Tennis courts are for playing tennis
not swearing oaths //

FERSEN. I agree //

MARIE. (Practicing your // backhand)

LOUIS. Well it's // crazy

FERSEN. And did you hear there are aristocrats
voluntarily turning over their estates
to be redistributed to the peasants //

MARIE. Ok well that's a bit much Isn't there some other
solution A stopgap?

LOUIS. I'm chary of making any concessions:

MARIE. *No you shouldn't.*

FERSEN. "Give them an // inch"

LOUIS. Or maybe it's a powderkeg and I'm helping to
foment revolution!?

MARIE. Well then play nice –

LOUIS. I did I met with the assemblies –

MARIE. So:

LOUIS. And it backfired!

FERSEN. So they're not to be trusted.

LOUIS. *(angry)* They just seem so ANGRY //

MARIE. Yes Well it's a *mob* //

LOUIS. *(insecure)* Maybe Turgot was right and I should've
taxed landed wealth //

MARIE. And then you FIRED him! //

LOUIS. *(tiny)* You think that was // unjust?

MARIE. I – DON'T – KNOW – // – LOUIS!!!

LOUIS. *(wringing his hands nervously)* He said if we taxed everyone only a few ducats more that'd avert bankruptcy.

MARIE. We aren't bankrupt.

FERSEN. Actually the public debt has tripled,

MARIE. Since when?

FERSEN. Past few years //

MARIE. *And it's my fault* //

LOUIS. No one's blaming // you

MARIE. They *aren't* What are you in*sensate* You didn't feel the *hostility* in the room?

LOUIS. It was general –

MARIE. It was directed AT ME They're gunning for ME.

(pause)

MARIE. I just don't know what these people want from me I'm a lesbian I'm a prostitute –

LOUIS. You can't please everyone //

MARIE. (You're right and you know what I can't deal with this my *son* is ill.)

FERSEN. Charles?

MARIE. Joseph he's //

FERSEN. What's wrong?

(beat)

MARIE. He'll be fine // it's

FERSEN. He's alright?

(beat)

MARIE. It's just a bit overwhelming.

FERSEN. *(concern)* Is there anything // I can

MARIE. *(attack)* HE'LL BE FINE.

(beat)

LOUIS. She's under a lot of stress.

FERSEN. I'm on your side Marie.

(beat)

MARIE. *(relaxes a bit)* Unlike Lafayette

    I can't believe he spearheaded this thing.

FERSEN. He's very seduced by American Ideas //

LOUIS. *(snarky)* "America" //

MARIE. That's true he's gone gaga;

FERSEN. But you supported America.

MARIE. *(innocuous)* When?

LOUIS. We signed a treaty.

MARIE. *(tantrum)* WE-DIDN'T-KNOW-WHAT-THE-HELL-THAT-WAS-LOUIS //

FERSEN. Uh //

MARIE. Now they're drawing up constitutions on the *tennis court?*

LOUIS. It's // insane

MARIE. They're challenging your divine right to monarchy – yes it *is* insane – and they're propounding this this //

LOUIS. Why can't we just do something?

MARIE. We what do you mean WE.

LOUIS. Me and you.

MARIE. No not "me and you" I don't have any agency here – I can't cut down on my clothes anymore I can't wear *burlap* It's *your* turn to *act.*

    (LOUIS starts fidgeting, trying to quell panic.)

LOUIS. I

    I. I could call troops?

FERSEN. That's a good idea.

LOUIS. Really?

FERSEN. Contain opposition Why not?

    (Beat. He's more emboldened.)

LOUIS. You know like Troops yeah like get a *concentration* of – all over Versailles?

    (Pause.)

    (He looks to FERSEN for affirmation. He gets nothing.)

(He looks to **MARIE** *for affirmation. He gets nothing.)*

(He bites his nails. He panics.)

LOUIS. And uh… also… *(ad hoc)* what about Paris?

*(***FERSEN*** *and* **MARIE** *consider this.)*

LOUIS. Paris yes Paris Is that.
Isn't that a good *idea?*

MARIE. Well it's something.

LOUIS. You think it's a solution?

MARIE. Try it.

(beat)

LOUIS. *(panic attack)* Ok.

(He won't leave.)

LOUIS. *(sickly smile)* But it's a
Really good idea right?

MARIE. *(tense smile)* Unless you want to accede to their reforms.

LOUIS. *(he bites his nails)* Right. No //

MARIE. Don't bite your nails.

LOUIS. I //

MARIE. *(hurrying him along)* Better get going //

FERSEN. *(supportive)* Bye!
[STOP]

LOUIS. You // don't think

MARIE. *(hysterical, jarring)* JUST – DO – IT – ALREADY!!

*(***LOUIS*** *exits abruptly;* **MARIE** *throws herself down on the divan, exhales.)*

(A long recuperative silence; pace slows considerably, it's more intimate. **FERSEN** *looks over to her.)*

FERSEN. I read it you know.

MARIE. What.

FERSEN. Your "autobiography."

MARIE. (Oh god.)

FERSEN. *(not titillated; ironic)* You've been very naughty.

MARIE. Yes but I've expiated my sins evidently.

> *(pause)*
>
> I can't believe what's happening Axel
> people are walking around *sans culottes*
> they're burning us in effigy
> it's gone haywire.

FERSEN. The whole thing will quash itself.
> Tempers flare and then they die out and things go
> back to normal. *(beat)* It's just a lot of noise.
>
> *(pause)*

MARIE. I've been having nightmares
> Last night I was eaten by a pack of wolves…
>
> *(She breaks down all at once. He goes to her.)*

MARIE. *(very vulnerable)* I'm sorry
> It's
> it's just that my *son* is really sick? everything
> is coming at me all at once //

FERSEN. It's a lot of // pressure

MARIE. I feel like I'm inside a gyroscope All that – spinning
> you know And the axis and – no gravity to hold it in
> place.
>
> *(beat)*

FERSEN. What happened to my butterfly queen?

MARIE. *(wipes her tears)* Oh god She's back in the chrysalis
> //

FERSEN. No //

MARIE. *(playing)* Yes reverting to her caterpillar state and all
> ready to crawl back to Austria for a Linzer tart.

FERSEN. *(small laugh)* Give me a break //

MARIE. I'm serious.

FERSEN. You've never *crawled* in your life.

MARIE. (some of the old impudence, but it's endearing)
> Well that's true.

(They laugh; it subsides. Pause. Quiet. **MARIE** *is increasingly fearful again.)*

MARIE. *(a fearful confession)* This man? he accosted me at the assembly, he was in all black A peasant probably.

It was very ominous.

His face was like a bullet:

And he said to me:

"You think *this* is bad? *this* is just a preamble to your suffering."

(Beat; she snaps out of it. She artifices a queenly smile. She offers him chocolates from a box.)

MARIE. Dark or light?

FERSEN. They're just trying to scare you.

MARIE. Je ne sais pas.

FERSEN. *(rueful)* People will do anything to get power.

8.

(MARIE pacing frantically, her boudoir, Petit Trianon.)

(LAMBALLE is looking after the DAUPHIN.)

MARIE. And I've lost all my friends, so much for my "coterie" –

LAMBALLE. (I feel like I'm not getting much // credit)

MARIE. *(not hearing her)* Ignominious pricks They pack off and leave without so much as a word //

LAMBALLE. Who //

MARIE. The Polignacs Count of Artois INGRATES //

DAUPHIN. Maman? //

MARIE. *(snaps)* Laissez moi //

LAMBALLE. (I'll watch him) //

MARIE. (No-stay-here-with-me-I'm-freakin-out) //

LAMBALLE. I'll get you a glass of water //

MARIE. I'M – NOT – THIRSTY.

   (pause)

LAMBALLE. *(starting to lose patience)* Please calm down //

MARIE. I'm not stupid I know what's happening – there's riots all over the city Lamballe – Where is Louis he was supposed to be here yesterday I haven't heard a thing //

LAMBALLE. Where'd he go //

MARIE. Paris I – DON'T YOU LISTEN TO ANYTHING I SAY he dispatched troops weeks ago //

LAMBALLE. Maybe he got // delayed

MARIE. That should've put an end to it //

LAMBALLE. He's probably //

MARIE. "Probably" I don't tarry in probabilities Therese I need to know what's happening //

LAMBALLE. *(snaps, shouts at her)* I DON'T KNOW WHAT TO SAY.

   (MARIE's chastened. She sighs, penitent.)

MARIE. I know I'm being totally crazy right now I know that.

And I know there's something I should be doing, to rectify all this but I don't know what it is. Do you know? What is it?

LAMBALLE. Some things are out of your control.

MARIE. *(snaps) Well that's not good enough.*

LAMBALLE. WELL THAT'S WHAT I HAVE TO OFFER YOU!

(pause)

MARIE. I'm *trying*. I *am*. but maybe there's something I don't see, I don't know some kind of blind spot? and I can't seem to overcome it?

(beat)

LAMBALLE. *(oddly direct)* Maybe you're right.

MARIE. I don't know what to do.

LAMBALLE. *(more gingerly)* You're grieving.

You lost a child.

He only just died.

MARIE. *(very tiny) But I should be responsible.*

LAMBALLE. You're a queen. You're not exempt from misfortune.

MARIE. Maybe I neglect them

I don't know my mother neglected me To me it's normal.

(pause)

Do you know when I got to Versailles mother spied on me She did. *(beat)* Spied on me and punished and exhorted me and never raised me.

(She's submerged in a mental fog.)

Sometimes I feel like... I'm not even a...person...

(pause; then demurring)

Do you ever feel that way?

(A pause as **LAMBALLE** *attempts to hide her own deeply uncomfortable recognition.)*

LAMBALLE. *(bluntly)* No.

MARIE. I'm sure I'm just upset. And you're right. It should all be fine.

(a weird silence)

*(***LOUIS*** enters. He's wearing the tricolor cockade in his hat, we instantly know something's deeply wrong.)*

MARIE. What happened?

LOUIS. I had to send them back.

MARIE. *(incredulous)* What is that.

(He doesn't answer.)

MARIE. What IS that?

(She rips the cockade from his hat.)

MARIE. *(rising slowly)* Are you crazy?

LOUIS. There was a huge mob. They wanted – I don't know, *gunpowder?*

MARIE. *Gun*powder? What // are you

LOUIS. They came from the Invalides,

MARIE. What mob? Where? Where // are you

LOUIS. They broke in there, they-they got all these *guns* and um //

MARIE. WHAT MOB?

LOUIS. The Bastille – there was a whole – they killed all these people //

MARIE. WHO? //

LOUIS. They dragged the governor into the streets, they they stabbed him, they s-*sawed* off his head. And. It's… I don't know, there's…a new city *government…?*

*(***MARIE*** reacts. **LAMBALLE** covers her mouth.)*

LOUIS. *(re: the cockade)* I had to.

[STOP]

MARIE. Therese you should go //

LOUIS. *(a boy)* I'm // scared.

MARIE. *(taking the dauphin)* I'll take him LEAVE //

LAMBALLE. But

Will you be // alright?

MARIE. YES JUST GO.

(**THERESE** *is paralyzed.*)

MARIE. *(increasingly worried)* LEAVE.

LAMBALLE. But I

I can't // just

MARIE. YES YOU CAN JUST *LEAVE!*

(**THERESE** *exits. The lights shift. A riot*)

[**TITLE**: A MOB OF THOUSANDS GATHERS IN PARIS AND MARCHES ON VERSAILLES]

[**TITLE**: THEY DISCOVER A GATE TO THE PALACE IS UNLOCKED]

[**TITLE**: THEY STORM THE PALACE AND SEARCH FOR THE QUEEN]

[**TITLE**: A RIOT]

9.

(Versailles. It's wrecked.)

(MARIE is holding suitcases. LOUIS has just entered the room. They're looking away from each other. A tableau.)

(silence)

MARIE. I had them pack our things.

LOUIS. We can't leave.

(She turns to him.)

MARIE. Everyone's escaped but *us //*

LOUIS. But I think it might be worse
　　If we tried to escape don't you think?

MARIE. *(flabbergasted)* HOW?
　　HOW can it be WORSE?
　　They threatened to roast me on a *spit.*

LOUIS. Don't be outré.

MARIE. OUTRE??!
　　They want to EAT me *//*

LOUIS. No *//*

MARIE. Literally: Yes! they were saying things like "I want the thigh meat! I want the leg!" I had to get out on the balcony.

LOUIS. What did you say?

MARIE. I feel your pain (and then I curtsied).

LOUIS. *That's* convincing.

MARIE. *Well* it was the best I could muster *//*

LOUIS. *(mollifying)* Of *// course*

MARIE. And you don't KNOW Louis They still LIKE you
　　To them I'm just some bitch from Austria who gives
　　everyone *blowjobs //*

LOUIS. Please keep your comportment *//*

MARIE. It's true *//*

LOUIS. You're still *//* a queen

MARIE. And I'm *keeping* my comportment Do you know what I was doing as they waved their hatchets at me and threw rocks?

(She waves a queenlike wave and smiles a frozen smile.)

LOUIS. *(approbation)* That's *very* regal.

(She gives him a look.)

LOUIS. *What?*

(She's thinking "this is really my life, oh god")

MARIE. Play with your clocks I'm going back to Austria.

(She grabs suitcases.)

LOUIS. Wait a minute let's just think this through.

MARIE. No! No more indecision!

LOUIS. I CAN'T JUST LEAVE
I HAVE A RESPONSIBILITY.

(She eyeballs him.)

MARIE. You have a *responsibility*.
To *me*.

LOUIS. I can't just abandon everything.

*(***MARIE*** *looks at him, helplessly.)*

MARIE. Then stay.

(She picks up the suitcases.)

LOUIS. You're leaving?

MARIE. Yes.

(pause)

LOUIS. You're going to leave me?

(short pause)

MARIE. *(not flip)* It's been nice Louis.
But I've never been in love with you.
And I won't be undone by you. Sorry.

(pause)

LOUIS. Oh.

(pause)

MARIE. *(now feels awful)* You're not coming?

LOUIS. I just

I

I need to think.

*(**MARIE** holds her suitcases, looking at him.)*

(She's about to walk out.)

*(**LOUIS** is completely rudderless.)*

Fuck.

(She can't do it.)

(She puts the suitcases down.)

*(**LOUIS** buries his head in her breast and weeps.)*

10.

(A **REVOLUTIONARY** *appears, accosts* **MARIE.***)*

REVOLUTIONARY. Necklace:

(She removes her necklace with difficulty; hands it to him.)

Rings:

(She reluctantly removes her rings.)

MARIE. Who will draw my bath.

REVOLUTIONARY. Bracelets:

MARIE. I'm tired.

REVOLUTIONARY. Hairpiece:

MARIE. You don't need to take that.

(He looks up at her.)

MARIE. *(a bitch)* I don't see why I should give you anything –

(He rips it off her head, she screams.)

[STOP]

MARIE. Where are my servants.

REVOLUTIONARY. Gone.

MARIE. Who will draw my bath.

REVOLUTIONARY. You will not bathe
You have been stripped of the privilege.

MARIE. I feel ill:
where // is

REVOLUTIONARY. Shh //

MARIE. *(rage)* DON'T SHUSH ME –

(He slaps her. Hard.)

REVOLUTIONARY. *(quiet but in her face)*
You know what I see when I look at you?
Bracelets:
Silk:
A hairdo.

[STOP]

MARIE. *(humiliated but trying to stay regal)* This is all a bit *de trop* don't you think?

(He grabs her by the throat.)

REVOLUTIONARY. *(looking through her)* You don't understand.
It's not the same.
It's not the same
Anymore.

(She nods, slowly, acquiescent, a harrowing understanding.)

End of Act One

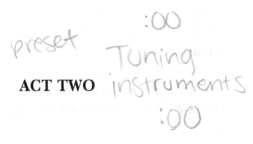

preset :00
Tuning
instruments
:00

ACT TWO

1.
[TITLE: 1791]

(The Tuileries)

*(**MARIE** is doing needlepoint.)*

*(The **DAUPHIN** is bored.)*

MARIE. Go play in the gardens There's mazes.

DAUPHIN. I want to see Paris.

MARIE. You can get lost.

DAUPHIN. I don't want to play in the gardens.

MARIE. You're being very naughty.

DAUPHIN. *(insulted)* I'm *not* naughty.

MARIE. You can't see Paris now.

DAUPHIN. Why?

MARIE. Because we're in the Tuileries, isn't it lovely?

　　(beat)

DAUPHIN. Which arrondisement are we in?

MARIE. Go off and play,

DAUPHIN. I don't *like* the Tuileries //

MARIE. Now //

DAUPHIN. *(tantrum)* I DON'T WANT TO PLAY IN THE GARDENS!

　　(STOP. He looks at her: an impasse.)

　　*(**LOUIS** enters.)*

LOUIS. Smashing game of billiards //

57

MARIE. (We have to talk) //

LOUIS. *(re: her handiwork)* Needlepoint?

MARIE. Louis:

LOUIS. What is it, a jug?

MARIE. We have to get out of here.

LOUIS. What do you think I'd been *planning* //

MARIE. Shh put this on. — *tea*

(She produces a farmer's outfit.)

LOUIS. What is it.

MARIE. A disguise.

LOUIS. Where'd you get that.

MARIE. We're going to Varennes.

LOUIS. What *is* this?!

MARIE. *(hurriedly applying his fake mustache)* We're farmers.

(She puts on her farmer costume.)

MARIE. It's all arranged, General Bouille will meet us there and we'll be safe, there's an army, and we can escape at the border.

(She looks at him, fixes his hat; they look crazy.)

MARIE. There:

LOUIS. How do I look?

(beat)

MARIE. *(perfunctory)* Yeah It looks good Come on –

2.

(The carriage)

(On the way to Varennes)

MARIE. We've been riding forever,

LOUIS. We're almost there,

MARIE. It's cramped, I need to stretch.

DAUPHIN. I have to pee.

LOUIS. Can you hold it?

DAUPHIN. I think so //

MARIE. Now where are we?

LOUIS. St. Menehould //

MARIE. (Ugh my back) //

LOUIS. We're almost there,

DAUPHIN. I can't hold it!

LOUIS. Let's not stop til we get to Varennes.

MARIE. "Stop the carriage" *(It'll just be for a second)* //

LOUIS. We're almost there.

(It stops.)

MARIE. *(to* **DAUPHIN***)* Go and pee darling //

LOUIS. *Marie –*

(They dismount the carriage. **DAUPHIN** *runs off,* **MARIE** *stretches.* **LOUIS** *takes a brief survey of the landscape.)*

LOUIS. Why is it like this?

MARIE. Like what?

LOUIS. *(making a face)* Rocks and things.

MARIE. It's called nature.

LOUIS. I know what nature is.

MARIE. You've led a very protected existence
   This is real life.

LOUIS. I know what real life is I'm not saying that,

MARIE. When I lived in Austria // I

LOUIS. "The danube, the shepherds" //

MARIE. Al*right* You don't have to be derisory I'm just saying //

LOUIS. *Je m'en fiche.*

MARIE. (Don't be *crude*)

LOUIS. (I learned how to curse)

MARIE. *(brushing it off)* You're crabby.

(She sits on the ground.)

Oh look a little earthworm. You know you can chop these up into a million pieces They're indestructible. I always liked nature. *(She looks around.)* Look darling there's a windmill. It's like the one I had built at *l'hameau.*

LOUIS. There's not many variations on windmills.

MARIE. What do they do, do you think.

LOUIS. Windmills?

(He shrugs.)

They're ornamental.

MARIE. Don't they have a function?

LOUIS. Beauty's a function.

(MARIE laughs.)

MARIE. You're so shallow.

(MARIE laughs.)

LOUIS. *I'm* shallow?

MARIE. There's more to life then glittery things dear //

LOUIS. *(umbrage)* Yes I *know* that //

MARIE. *(teasingly)* You're just so incredibly cosseted,

LOUIS. I can hardly accept that sort of indictment from the likes // of you

MARIE. *(sharp turn)* I CUT BACK I TOLD YOU THAT A MILLION TIMES!

(a tense pause)

LOUIS. *(looks away)* Anyway the damage is done.

(beat)

MARIE. "Damage."

(He doesn't answer.)

MARIE. Well that was below the belt Thanks.

(After a long pause, the DAUPHIN enters.)

DAUPHIN. Daddy I'm hungry.

LOUIS. We're nearly there Be patient,

MARIE. Did you pee.

(DAUPHIN nods.)

LOUIS. *(to MARIE)* Shall we?

MARIE. *(still smarting)* My back's killing me Help me up.

(They're about to get back in the carriage. MARIE spies something in the distance.)

MARIE. Oh wait there's someone //

LOUIS. *Let's go, // quickly*

MARIE. *"Excusez moi"* //

LOUIS. (What are you doing –

MARIE. I want to ask them something) "Helloo?"

(SAUCE, the shopkeeper, enters with his wife.)

SAUCE. Hi.

MARIE. *Bon jour.* Or. I mean "hi" – well I don't know but //

MRS SAUCE. Hi //

MARIE. (Yes hi) Would you mind resolving an argument between my husband and me, we were wondering: What do windmills do Are they just decorative or do they have a function? Or:

(beat)

SAUCE. Windmills.

MARIE. Yes.

(beat)

MRS SAUCE. Aren'tcha farmers?

LOUIS. *(takes her by the arm)* She's just // kidding

MARIE. *(impromptu, pulls away)* We are farmers but you see we're very new farmers We're sort of neophytes and we don't know all the technicalities.

(**SAUCE** *and* **MRS SAUCE** *exchange looks.*)

SAUCE. You grind things.

(beat)

MARIE. What?

MRS SAUCE. *Windmills.*

MARIE. O.

SAUCE. You grind things.

MARIE. O So they *do* have a function //

LOUIS. *(tries to get **MARIE** in the carriage)* Well you were right That solves // that Ok bye

MARIE. *(magnetized to them)* Do you live around here? HOLD ON A SECOND (What an interesting frock) //

(**MARIE** *feels her frock.*)

MRS SAUCE. Thank // you

MARIE. If you don't mind my asking are you in a business of some kind? Or //

SAUCE. We're shopkeepers //

MARIE. *(delighted) Shop*keepers! *R*eally!

SAUCE. We're right down that road.

MARIE. *(takes them by the arm)* And what does that involve?

(earnest)

I mean – like What sort of life is it?

Is it

Spiritually nourishing?

(They look at her.)

MARIE. I mean…do you feel like a…real…*person*?

SAUCE. *(suspicious; to* **LOUIS***)* You look familiar //

DAUPHIN. Maman I'm *hun*gry,

SAUCE. Where've I seen you?

(He and MRS SAUCE *exchange a look.)*

LOUIS. We *really should* be going. Darling?

*(*LOUIS *extends his hand to her.* MRS SAUCE *grabs her arm.)*

SAUCE. *(stalling)* I'm Sauce and that's Mrs Sauce.

*(*MARIE *is a little unnerved.)*

MARIE. Hi.

MRS SAUCE. Hi.

(lots of smiling)

MARIE. Well: it was *so* lovely to meet you
I'm sure // we'll

DAUPHIN. I'm hungry!

MRS SAUCE. Awwwww who's this sweet thing.
"He-llo"
"He-llo"

*(*SAUCE *approaches him.)*

SAUCE. You hungry, Little Man?

DAUPHIN. We're going to Varennes.

SAUCE. Varennes That's pretty far.

MRS SAUCE. It's getting dark come spend the night Chez Nous.

LOUIS. No That's ok.

SAUCE. You can't let your boy go hungry,
"Do you like potatoes?" //

DAUPHIN. *(shy)* I like meat //

SAUCE. *(pinches his cheeks)* Awwww //

DAUPHIN. Ow!

SAUCE. We have a room above the shop.

MRS SAUCE. We can teach you about shop-keeping.

SAUCE. You can have a nice sleep rest your little toesies.

(**SAUCE** *grabs* **DAUPHIN,** *it's somewhat violent, clutches him. A terrifying pause.*)

DAUPHIN. *(tiny, scared)* Maman?

(pause)

SAUCE. I'll take your luggage.

3.

(In the scene change, they remove their disguises.)

(They are back at the Tuileries.)

(MARIE's hair has turned white.)

LOUIS. "Windmills."

MARIE. At least we got to see a shop.

LOUIS. Now what.

MARIE. There's sentinels everywhere; there's men watching me undress, watching me sleep. It's much worse //

DAUPHIN. I want to go to Paris //

MARIE. (Mummy has a migraine darling) *Louis please do something,* I can not live in a prison //

LOUIS. We're alive aren't we.

MARIE. Barely,

LOUIS. I'm trying to think //

MARIE. You have to act not think They'll kill us in our // sleep

(A REVOLUTIONARY edges in and listens openly.)

LOUIS. We have to b –

(He stops – looks up at the REVOLUTIONARY.)

LOUIS. *(smiling tautly)* Hello.

REVOLUTIONARY 2. Hi.

(beat)

LOUIS. We're, uh: trying to have a *private* conversation?

REVOLUTIONARY 2. That's not allowed.

MARIE. *(taut smile)* What do you mean it's not allowed //

REVOLUTIONARY 2. You may only converse with one another in the presence of guards.

MARIE. Really, why's that?

REVOLUTIONARY 2. Now that you've run away you're considered *émigrés.*

LOUIS. What?

REVOLUTIONARY 2. Enemies of the state.

(pause)

MARIE. I see.

REVOLUTIONARY 2. Sorry.

(fake sheepish smile)

MARIE. So: forgive me I'm a bit dense Let me recap: we *run* the state: but we're *enemies* of the state.

REVOLUTIONARY 2. Yes.

(beat)

MARIE. Well that makes a ton of // sense.

REVOLUTIONARY 2. There's a revolution //

MARIE. A *revolution fine* but can't we have a private Conversation //

REVOLUTIONARY 2. No.

[STOP]

MARIE. Well: I realize we're prisoners and everything but we're going to need *some* privacy. And that's just how it *is*.

REVOLUTIONARY 2. No.

(MARIE looks at him, flaring insolence.)

MARIE. "No"

(REVOLUTIONARY chuckles, looks away.)

MARIE. *(temper flaring)*

I've made my life public for *your* delectation and *your* scrutiny and you won't allow *me* a private conversation with my own *husband*?

REVOLUTIONARY 2. No.

MARIE. That's kind of you, this "revolution" is very civilized.

REVOLUTIONARY 2. Civilization's a luxury we can't afford.

MARIE. What do we get in its stead? lopped heads and fresh-cut THROATS?

LOUIS. Marie:

MARIE. *(to* **LOUIS***)* NO, I'M SORRY, MY HAIR'S TURNED *WHITE!*

REVOLUTIONARY 2. *(quoting)* Terror without virtue is disastrous

and virtue without terror is impossible //

MARIE. *(covering her face in frustration)* Whatever //

DAUPHIN. I'm hungry //

REVOLUTIONARY 2. We've written a constitution // *"liberte*

MARIE. (Marvelous) //

REVOLUTIONARY 2. *Egalite // Fraternite"*

MARIE. *(indignation)* Yeah yeah stop blathering My son wants a *flan* or something can't we get a decent *meal?* //

REVOLUTIONARY 2. A decent *meal* //

MARIE. *Yes* a decent *meal* We're very *hungry* //

REVOLUTIONARY 2. I could starve you to death if I wanted.

MARIE. *Excuse* // me

REVOLUTIONARY 2. I could snap your necks and I'd get a standing ovation.

MARIE. *What.*

(She lifts her hand to strike him, **LOUIS** *stops her.)*

LOUIS. She's tired.

(She shakes **LOUIS** *off; stares the* **REVOLUTIONARY** *down.)*

MARIE. *(frightened but hiding it)* You're not some acolyte of enlightenment you know.

You're very young and you don't know much of anything.

REVOLUTIONARY 2. And you're very *old.*

MARIE. I'm thirty seven // It's

REVOLUTIONARY 2. OLDER.

MARIE. What are you talking about.

REVOLUTIONARY 2. The *Ancien Regime.*

MARIE. You don't make any sense //

REVOLUTIONARY 2. Maybe the sense can be knocked into your head once we've sliced it off your neck.

(He's scared her.)

LOUIS. Don't speak to my wife like that.

REVOLUTIONARY 2. Don't tell me how to speak
As if I'm to have reverence for you.

(The **REVOLUTIONARY** *spits in* **LOUIS'** *face.)*

LOUIS. I'm still your king.

REVOLUTIONARY 2. No you are shit; And you will die so France can live.

(pause; **LOUIS** *wipes off the spit.)*

LOUIS. I don't see it as so mutually exclusive.

REVOLUTIONARY 2. That's not me It's Robespierre,

MARIE. Oh // god

LOUIS. That *dandy?*

REVOLUTIONARY 2. He's not a dandy and his panegyrics on the system of revolutionary government and his praise of virtue // show

MARIE. "Virtue" o SHUT UP!

REVOLUTIONARY 2. how the system // of

MARIE. Can't he just have a nice little provincial practice as a LAWYER?

(no response)

MARIE. Well. Good for him. Okay then.

*(***REVOLUTIONARY** *doesn't leave.)*

MARIE. Bye.

(He doesn't leave.)

MARIE. *(to* **LOUIS***; bitter sarcasm)* He's *very* charming.

LOUIS. He spat in my face.

MARIE. *(terribly cutting)* Yes but there's a way of spitting in someone's face and being charming at the same time:

(beat)

it's a *talent.*

Like *juggling.*

(She smiles a fake smile at the **REVOLUTIONARY** *who smiles back, equally fake.)*

4.

(The Tuileries)

(**MARIE** – *with a tin of biscuits* – *is working feverishly on some kind of makeshift espionage.*)

LOUIS. Billiards?

MARIE. *(distracted)* No.

LOUIS. What's that?

MARIE. Cipher.

LOUIS. *(perked up)* What do you mean Like a *code?* //

MARIE. Shh, they'll hear –

LOUIS. In a box of *biscuits?* //

MARIE. *Can it.*

LOUIS. Since when do you know how to write in *cipher* //

MARIE. *(feverish)* (I'm-not-dying-in-the-fuckin-tuileries-that's-for-fuckin-certain-we're-getting-the-*fuck*-out-of-here!) //

LOUIS. What's going on //

MARIE. (Go play billiards) //

LOUIS. *(snooping in the box)* Are there any biscuits left? //

MARIE. *(wrests box, slaps hand)* Louis! //

LOUIS. (Or.) //

MARIE. *(stage whisper)* Did you know that 800 men from Marseilles have arrived and the deputies of the Jacobin clubs?

LOUIS. And?

MARIE. It's a pretty blunt gesture don't you think They're out to destroy us, openly, there's no pretense anymore, *at all.*

LOUIS. Where'd you hear this?

MARIE. Fersen.

LOUIS. He's *alive?*

MARIE. We've been writing each other.

LOUIS. *That's dangerous* //

MARIE. SHHH!

LOUIS. That's what you've been sewing into hatlinings? //

MARIE. *(gleeful)* (And I do it with pinpricks as well It's a kind of code)

LOUIS. *(delighted) No!*

MARIE. *(looks around, nervous) You think they saw me?*

LOUIS. You're ingenious //

MARIE. (I can't tell if I'm being paranoid or judicious.)

LOUIS. Why didn't you tell me?

MARIE. Because you're *apathetic* //

LOUIS. I'M NOT APATHETIC //

MARIE. *(whisper) Shut up!*

(*We hear the faint sound of church bells gonging.*)

LOUIS. I hate when you say that, I'm just *thinking:* biding my *options* We don't want to be feckless //

MARIE. I think it's a bit late for "feckless."

(**LOUIS** *hears the bells. Puzzled, turns to* **MARIE.**)

LOUIS. What's going on?

(**MARIE** *reacts.*)

MARIE. *Oh my god…*

LOUIS. What.

MARIE. You're not gonna believe it: Fersen told the Duke of Brunswick about us And he sent this letter to the Jacobins saying that if they do even the smallest violence to us the whole city of Paris will be *destroyed!*

LOUIS. So:

MARIE. Don't you see? we're getting out of here.

LOUIS. We are?

MARIE. You think they'd let it escalate to that? We're getting out of here!

(beat)

(*They do a little dance of excitement.* **ROYALIST** *walks in on them.*)

ROYALIST. Sire //

LOUIS. *(caught dancing)* Yes what is it.

ROYALIST. I'm. sorry to disrupt // your

LOUIS. That's quite alright.

ROYALIST. I. Have some unfortunate news
I'm afraid //

MARIE. *(claps her hands together w ersatz delight)* Ooh a change of pace how tonic.

LOUIS. What's the matter?

ROYALIST. There's riots everywhere; prisons are being opened everyone's getting hacked to pieces it's a nightmare.

(pause)

LOUIS. Oh.

(pause)

ROYALIST. They're trying to frighten the royalists evidently.

LOUIS. Are we safe?

ROYALIST. Word is they're going to converge on the Tuileries next.

(MARIE smiles.)

MARIE. *(flirtatious good humor)* But that can't happen.

ROYALIST. *(to LOUIS)* I fear they'll kill you if you // stay

MARIE. *(total denial)* (No darling it's a mistake of some kind) You must have some Misinformation.

ROYALIST. I'm afraid not your // majesty

MARIE. *(cracking somewhat) You listen to me.*
The Duke of Brunswick has *vowed* to protect us Do you understand the *magnitude* of the consequences if his orders are breeched?

LOUIS. *(to MARIE, tentative)* Maybe it backfired.

ROYALIST. Forgive me. But. I must ask you both to take refuge on the assembly.

(MARIE looks up.)

MARIE. The *assembly*.

> *(She laughs.)*

ROYALIST. *(discomfited by her)* They're meeting at the old riding grounds //

MARIE. That would be the same assembly that took up residence on our tennis courts and wants us DEAD *That* assembly?

ROYALIST. I know how it must // sound

MARIE. And they're to be our *refuge*.

ROYALIST. It's for your own good your // majesty

MARIE. *(breaking comportment)* My own good?

> Are you *joking*?

ROYALIST. It is your best // hope

MARIE. Are you *kidding*?

LOUIS. *(to MARIE)* It does seem dire //

MARIE. *(filip of rage)* HE'S LYING.

LOUIS. You heard what he said They'll kill us if we stay.

> *(beat)*

MARIE. *(regains composure)* Then they'll have to kill me here.

LOUIS. I think we should listen to him.

MARIE. I'm going to take a nap.

LOUIS. *(grabs her arm as she leaves)* Wait a // minute I

MARIE. YOU SHUT UP if it weren't for you we wouldn't even be here in the first place *(get off me)* //

LOUIS. But we have // to

MARIE. *(breaks free) No,* you've made all the wrong choices for us, *unfailingly, every* time, I won't budge!

LOUIS. *(reaching for her)* I //

MARIE. Fuck off No You can nail me to the WALLS FIRST.

> *(The sound of glass shattering.)*

[**TITLE**: THE TUILERIES ARE INVADED]

[**TITLE**: 600 PEOPLE ARE SLAUGHTERED]

[**TITLE**: THE ROYAL FAMILY IS ESCORTED TO
THE ASSEMBLY]

[**TITLE**: THE MOB DESCENDS UPON THE
ASSEMBLY]

[**TITLE**: DEMANDING THE DEPOSITION OF
THE KING]

[**TITLE**: AND CUSTODY OF THE ROYAL
FAMILY]

5.

(The sound of rioting outside.)

(They're crowded in a tiny room sitting in terror.)

(It's hot.)

(MARIE paces.)

(Long silence.)

MARIE. I feel faint.

    (beat)

I feel faint.

LOUIS. Be still.

MARIE. It's sweltering and somebody stole my purse on the way.

DAUPHIN. I want to take a bath.

MARIE. This is torture.

    (She covers her ears. Long pause.)

MARIE. Why don't they kill us what are they waiting for.

LOUIS. They won't kill us.

MARIE. Won't they.

LOUIS. Listen to me: we'll get out of this.

    (MARIE says nothing.)

LOUIS. I know what you think of me
    But I promise you
    I'll get us out of this.

    (MARIE says nothing.)

LOUIS. Look at me.

MARIE. What.

    *(LOUIS sings a serenade to her – odd, sweet, funny –
    to the sounds of fighting, cannonfire, battlecries in the
    background.)*

LOUIS. "Un rêve jolie t'attend

Quand le sommeil t'en prend
Beaux rêves
Venez à mon bébé
Beaux rêves
Venez à mon bébé
La nuit approche, le jour finit
Endors-toi, petit chéri

Beaux rêves
Venez à mon bébé
Beaux rêves
Venez à mon bébé…"

(**LOUIS** *looks at her.*)

MARIE. That was off-key.

(*A beat. He breaks into laughter.*)

(*They all break into laughter.*)

(*The sounds of bullets and bloodshed over their laughter.*)

6.

(A holding cell.)

MARIE. Where is he.

(no answer)

MARIE. Where is my husband.

DAUPHIN. Maman //

MARIE. *(to guards)* WHY WON'T YOU TELL ME ANYTHING!

(long awful silence)

MARIE. "*Oh really that's so interesting.*"

DAUPHIN. *(softly, sad, apologetic)* (Maman, I do want to play in the gardens.)

(pause)

MARIE. *(ignoring **DAUPHIN**, to guard)* LOOK is he alive, dead, what.

(no answer)

DAUPHIN. *(tugging at her sleeve)* Maman?

(beat)

Maman //

MARIE. *WHAT:*

(beat)

DAUPHIN. *(demurs, she's scary)* I want to play in the gardens.

MARIE. *(strain)* Sweetheart
You can't play in the gardens
Now.

(pause)

DAUPHIN. *(tears; quiet)* I want to play in the // gardens

MARIE. DID YOU HEAR WHAT I SAID
YOU CAN'T PLAY IN THE GARDENS.

(pause)

DAUPHIN. Why?

MARIE. Because there's no gardens anymore.

DAUPHIN. Why //

MARIE. BECAUSE WE'RE PRISONERS.

(She falls apart, it's too much. The **DAUPHIN** *grabs onto her dress, frightened.)*

DAUPHIN. Don't cry.

(She doesn't answer.)

Don't //

MARIE. Will you get: OFF ME.

(She pushes him away from her, very violent.)

(Immediately she regrets this, realizes what she's done.)

(A guard picks up the **DAUPHIN**.*)*

GUARD. *(whispers to the other* **GUARD***)* Portez-le à l'autre salle.

(He carries off the **DAUPHIN**.*)*

MARIE. What are you doing
Where are you going *I didn't mean that.*
WHAT ARE YOU DOING WITH HIM, THAT'S MY SON!

(shaking, hysterical)

C-c-c-come back
Where are
Wh-wh-wh
Wh

*(***MARIE*** weeps and weeps. The lights darken.)*

(The sounds of water dripping.)

(We are underground, the conciergerie. A week or so later, but seamless.)

(From now through the end of the play the scenes should begin bleeding together. We should lose the sense of any clear demarcation between the beginnings and ends of scenes.)

(**SHEEP** *appears.*)

SHEEP. *Comment allez vous.*

MARIE. Sheep?

SHEEP. *Comment allez vous* Marie.

MARIE. What's happening to me?

SHEEP. I'm so sorry.

MARIE. I haven't seen you since that day, in the fields, at Trianon.

SHEEP. Yes, it's been a while.

MARIE. I don't even know what's become of Versailles.

SHEEP. Be careful Marie.

MARIE. Of what?

SHEEP. *(softly)* Don't go mad.

MARIE. I WON'T! My mother told me never to fear death so I'm very resolute.

SHEEP. Your hand is shaking.

MARIE. They separated the dauphin from me, out of spite, they put him in a cell beneath me, I could hear him crying for me. Then they moved me underground – but I don't know where I am…

SHEEP. The conciergerie.

MARIE. But they left my son in the Temple, do you know what's happened to him?

SHEEP. No I'm just a sheep.

(She looks at him. She laughs.)

MARIE. Oh my god This is a comedy.

SHEEP. Baaa.

MARIE. *(wipes her eyes)* Well it's better than nothing.

[STOP]

MARIE. Do you know I begged them to let him stay? *Begged* them. But the minister laughed at me, "you Austrian whore why do you feign love for this bastard" – it's so funny I'm an AUSTRIAN whore I love the qualifiers – as if AUSTRIAN makes me somehow more lurid Like I'm MORE whorish because I'm Austrian.

[STOP]

MARIE. (They were happy to have me when I was a queen) I'M STILL A FUCKING QUEEN!!

(pause; she's embarrassed, tries to retract.)

MARIE. *(forcing hope)* The Austrian army has crossed the border of France They're forty leagues from Paris, surely they will come for me. I'm still royal there. They have to come for me. Don't they?

SHEEP. You look exhausted.

MARIE. I can't get any rest; I close my eyes and just lie there.

SHEEP. It helps to count sheep.

(She looks at him.)

MARIE. One.

(beat)

SHEEP. Maybe it's better to count backwards //

MARIE. Backwards from one? //

SHEEP. Is this too abstract //

MARIE. Yes and you know I'm not good at abstract thinking; that's what Countess Brandeiss used to say.

SHEEP. You're better at concrete thinking? //

MARIE. The truth is I HATE thinking! I do, I have problems focussing – you know what I miss, I miss gambling, I miss my friends. I miss my little biscuit and espresso in the morning. *(beat)* You must think I'm acting all sorry for myself.

SHEEP. No.

MARIE. You're very understanding; Animals are so absolving.

SHEEP. Thank you.

MARIE. I miss nature.

*(A beat; **SHEEP** moves closer to her; very gingerly.)*

SHEEP. Rousseau believed in the primacy of human nature.

*(**MARIE** looks at him.)*

MARIE. Did he?

SHEEP. That people are good but society is a corrupting force.

(pause)

MARIE. Do you believe that?

(beat)

SHEEP. What do *you* believe?

(pause)

MARIE. *(to herself; a discovery)* I don't know.

*(**SHEEP** takes a step towards her.)*

SHEEP. You should have read Rousseau //

MARIE. *(echoing him)* I should've read Rousseau Voltaire; I should have memorized the maxims of La Rochefoucauld.

SHEEP. "We always love those who admire us, but we do not always love those whom we admire."

MARIE. *(trying to memorize as he speaks it)* Another:

SHEEP. "True love, however rare, is still more common than true friendship."

MARIE. Tell me more,

SHEEP. What about?

(beat)

MARIE. *(deeply sincere)* Teach me.

[STOP]

SHEEP. Are you familiar with Newton's work in physics?

MARIE. *(freaking out)* Who's he?

SHEEP. *(soft, gentle smile)* Isaac Newton proved how natural events conform to underlying laws. This showed people like Voltaire that nature could be used as a model for human society.

MARIE. Voltaire wanted to come see me at court but I refused him Should I invite him back?

SHEEP. Too late for that.

(beat)

MARIE. Trianon's gone, that's right,

SHEEP. And he's dead.

MARIE. They hacked him up?

SHEEP. Natural causes.

MARIE. And who's Isaac Newman?

SHEEP. Isaac *Newton* believed in an intelligible order that underlies all of nature //

MARIE. I agree with that.

(**SHEEP** *nods "no".*)

MARIE. I don't?

SHEEP. You believe in Absolute Monarchy.

MARIE. Well I'm the queen.

SHEEP. Monarchy has its roots in inequality.

MARIE. So:

SHEEP. Inequality is unnatural.

MARIE. What's the alternative?

(*a beat*)

SHEEP. Democracy.

(*Beat.* **MARIE** *laughs.* **SHEEP** *does not.* **MARIE** *looks at him.*)

MARIE. No really.

SHEEP. Now you've insulted me.

MARIE. *(struggling)* But common people can't take care of them*selves*. Democracy can't work.

SHEEP. Hierarchy cannot survive because it goes against the laws of nature //

MARIE. Yes & Democracy is godless rule.

SHEEP. Come now, you don't really believe in god.

MARIE. Sheep you're blasphemous.

SHEEP. *(gentle)* The only god is natural law. Reason.

(*long pause*)

MARIE. *(totally rudderless)* I don't know what to believe.

(pause)

SHEEP. *(hypnotic; an incantation)* Liberte, egalite, fraternite...

MARIE. *(recoiling)* Perhaps I should've treated my subjects with greater consideration I've tried to amend that. But Common People can't take care of themselves, they can't make decisions, they aren't *sovereign //*

SHEEP. *(sudden virulent shift, an attack)* NO – *YOU* CAN'T TAKE CARE OF *YOUR*SELF! *YOU* CAN'T MAKE DECISIONS! *YOU* AREN'T SOVEREIGN!

(pause)

MARIE. *(grasping at straws)* I'm queen of France.

(SHEEP *takes another step towards her.)*

MARIE. *(weakening, tired)* Just because something's modern doesn't make it true.

SHEEP. Use *Reason.*

MARIE. *(lost)* But I can't dispense with the past with history //

SHEEP. That's why you've become its victim.
And your own life was lost to you.

MARIE. *(He's right.)* I wish I could sleep.

SHEEP. Wake up.

[STOP; *the next section is to herself*]

MARIE. *(sad, exhaustion)* What did you say? Count backwards?

SHEEP. Negative numbers: negative one, two //

MARIE. I was bad at math.

(long pause)

MARIE. I feel so alone.

SHEEP. *(sweetly)* Pet me.

(A beat. She turns to him)

MARIE. Yes, I need to be close to someone.

SHEEP. "Ach du, meine kinder."

MARIE. German, I haven't heard it since I was little, come sheep //

SHEEP. Baa //

MARIE. Close to my heart.

(*As* **SHEEP** *approaches* **MARIE** *he sloughs off* **SHEEP** *skin, reveals himself to be a wolf. This is magic, and it's terrifying. The wolf attacks her. We hear the loud growling, her cries, her screams.*)

(**REVOLUTIONARY** *3 enters.*)

MARIE. (*disoriented*) How long have I been here.

(*The* **REVOLUTIONARY** *is preparing to shear her hair with a straight razor.*)

MARIE. Where's my son?

REVOLUTIONARY 3. I have orders not to speak with the widow Capet.

MARIE. "The: oh that's *me?*

I see.

(*He starts to cut.*)

MARIE. Not too short.

(*pause*)

I have fleas in my hair can I at least wash it?

(*He cuts.*)

Guess not.

(*He cuts.*)

"There once was a girl named Marie. whose head was infested with fleas –"

(*laughter*)

[STOP]

When's my trial Can you tell me that.

REVOLUTIONARY 3. Two weeks.

MARIE. Thank you.

(The waters of the Seine drip around them as he cuts her hair.)

MARIE. You can't understand it, but I was *born* to be a *queen.* It wasn't my *choosing,* I was born *into* it.

[STOP]

And I wasn't raised I was *built:* I was built to be this *thing,* and now they're killing me for it – but you'd be the same You'd make the same choices I did.

REVOLUTIONARY 3. And if you had my lot you'd choose the same as me.

(beat)

MARIE. What do you want

From me

REVOLUTIONARY 3. We want to institute new ways of living.

MARIE. *(makes a connection)* But I wanted the same *thing,*

REVOLUTIONARY 3. For *yourself* //

MARIE. That's //

REVOLUTIONARY 3. You think your bullshit pastoralism counts?

While you paraded around in your Peasant costume, *real* peasants were starving to death.

MARIE. Then I was wrong to do that! But is this how you exercise *virtue?* I don't *get* // it

REVOLUTIONARY 3. "Virtue without terror –

MARIE. *(exasperated)*

Is impossible *yeah I* // *know.*

REVOLUTIONARY 3. We want equality //

MARIE. Right //

REVOLUTIONARY 3. Can you understand // that

MARIE. I don't have to "understand it" It's been jammed down // my throat

REVOLUTIONARY 3. And to get that we will *destroy you.*

(He looks her in the eye.)

Do you understand?

You will be *eradicated.*

No one will *remember* you.

And when we're done it'll be like *you never existed.*

(He eyeballs her for a moment. Slowly, he makes his way behind her and resumes cutting.)

MARIE. *(grasping at straws)* But I had a right to be // queen

REVOLUTIONARY 3. Shut up.

MARIE. I ruled by divine – OW.

YOU CUT ME.

[STOP]

MARIE. *(sincerely pleading)* People's nature is *good,* isn't that what you believe, Rousseau? Isn't that what he says?

REVOLUTIONARY 3. You pervert Rousseau.

MARIE. Then tell me, what does he say?

Really, I want to know.

Teach me something, would you?

(hysterical) EDUCATE ME.

REVOLUTIONARY 3. I'm not supposed to speak to you.

MARIE. Why, you'll be arrested for treason?

REVOLUTIONARY 3. Head down.

MARIE. *(bitter)* Oh that's *liberty* //

REVOLUTIONARY 3. *Quiet* //

MARIE. Not so short.

(He cuts.)

REVOLUTIONARY 3. Poor thing

You act like everything's hurt you

And everyone's used you

And you're just some sweet sunburnt girl at the beach

You won't look at reality.

MARIE. "Reality."

REVOLUTIONARY 3. Pity.

MARIE. The reality is you can't have a *nation* without a *king.*

REVOLUTIONARY 3. What about America?

MARIE. *(practically in tears)* AMERICA:

I'm so *sick* of hearing about AMERICA:

America is a *doomed* experiment.

Don't you see *this will weaken France to the point of extinction?!*

REVOLUTIONARY 3. Democracy will give us what we need.

MARIE. But it *won't.* Look around you. People will just grab for what they can They just want *blood.*

(beat)

You think these people care about you?

REVOLUTIONARY 3. Sit down.

MARIE. You're nothing to them. You're dispensible. And when they don't need you anymore they'll leave you here to rot.

(beat)

They won't come for you.

They won't come for you.

You don't have anyone.

REVOLUTIONARY 3. *(a command)* S*it down.*

*(**MARIE** sits back down. The **REVOLUTIONARY** cuts. She laughs from the absurdity.)*

MARIE. Well what do I know I'm badly *educated;* what, you think I'm kidding? I'm practically fucking *illiterate* actually. these men of letters? these *Jacobins* they had more advantages than I ever did: EVER. *(beat)* Montesqieu Diderot they want you to use *reason:* well guess what? I *can't* reason! I can't do basic *math*! I can't make sense of my *life.* Now *what?*!

(He cuts, ignoring her.)

I was fourteen. I was shipped off to marry a rich French boy who couldn't even tuck his own *shirt* in, I was stripped of *everything.*

(He won't look at her; despair)

MARIE. I didn't know what else to *be*

Don't you underSTAND THAT?

(pause)

REVOLUTIONARY 3. Do you think

I can *save* you?

MARIE. No.

REVOLUTIONARY 3. Then why are you talking to me.

(He exits.)

(Time shifts.)

*(**MARIE** is alone in her cell.)*

(She's aged ten years at least. She's shaking uncontrollably. She's babbling – she's sometimes incoherent.)

MARIE. *(increasingly unstable)* November second

that's when I was born That's my birthday

all souls day Day of the dead

but I was bright and shining

fishermen on the Danube shepherds on the mountains

bright bright

then Charles died the smallpox

(beat; then overemphatic)

NO JOANNA

Joanna first then Charles

Joanna Charles *I can't remember all their names*

[STOP]

Thought I was being protected *how could she protect you*
it wasn't rational.

(defiant)

I'm NOT RATIONAL.

(beat; quiescent)

MARIE. Brokering marriages she was gone Forging alliances
Gone
France gone
Prussia she didn't give a *shit* "QUIET MARIE."

*(beat; she weeps; she stops; slaps herself violently; points
as if speaking to someone else)*

MARIE. "an archduchess does *not* shed tears in public."

(whispers to herself)

"Ja Mutter ich kuemmere mich um meine Aufgaben."*

[STOP]

*(We hear the waters of the Seine. She grabs her head in
agony.)*

MARIE. (the sounds are driving me crazy) STOP IT.
(I can't be in a cage) Oh god – I...I *can't* – be in a
cage...

*(There's an imperceptible shift in the room. FERSEN
appears. It should be dreamlike, ethereal.)*

FERSEN. Hello Marie.

(MARIE looks up at him, disbelieving)

MARIE. Fersen?

(She goes to him, tentative at first.)

MARIE. I thought they killed you.

FERSEN. No. I'm here.

MARIE. How'd you get in here?

FERSEN. Connections I'm Swedish.

*(She laughs, deep sadness, hugs him, holds him for dear
life.)*

MARIE. Oh this is a dream.

(After a moment, she pulls away.)

Fersen, we're not royal anymore: they killed Louis,
and they took my kids from me, and they won't tell me
what's happening.

---

* "Yes Mother I'll attend to my lessons"

FERSEN. Don't cry Marie.

MARIE. Sorry You're right, I mustn't forget my deportment.

(*She wipes her eyes hurriedly, assays her old charm.*)

I'd offer you a seat but I've only got this ratty straw mattress which you're welcome to if you don't mind lice.

(*She laughs.*)

FERSEN. (*smiling*) You look well.

MARIE. *Please*, I look terrible I *smell* terrible.

Look: these inguinal stains, my armpits, I can't stand my own stench. Actually you get used to it, the smells? piss shit they cancel themselves out; the senses putrefy – I'm just faking all this,

FERSEN. What?

MARIE. Hauteur? (I don't know) I have to hold on to *something*.

FERSEN. I don't blame you.

MARIE. You're the only one who doesn't.

FERSEN. You still have adherents.

MARIE. They have made me into something disgusting, with their pamphlets their smears –

(*beat*)

I wish they'd
kill me already //

FERSEN. (*pity*) Don't say that,

MARIE. Oh do let me be impious *please*.

(*beat*)

MARIE. There's been a trial;
I'm sure to be found guilty.

FERSEN. Of what.

MARIE. Believe me they'll come up with something. They're nothing if not industrious.

FERSEN. What does your lawyer say?

MARIE. *(frayed amusement)* Oh him? he was arrested for treason.

FERSEN. *What?*

MARIE. Yes I asked if he was tired and they thought we were getting *chummy.*

FERSEN. Oh no.

[STOP]

MARIE. *(sudden drop)* It's no use They want to saw me in half Like a tree Count the ringed interiors So I'll give it to them.

FERSEN. Don't give up.

(She's in a mental fog for a moment, then snaps out of it.)

MARIE. No

(trying to cultivate "hope")

No of *course* not, I'm very resolute!

(beat; then excited – but hypermetabolic)

MARIE. The Austrian army has crossed the border of France, did you know that, a while back? They'll come for me, don't you think? They *have* to. I just have to be patient and they'll come for me. They're my own *people* They'll come for me.

(beat)

OH: Look!

*(She produces something; hands it to **FERSEN**.)*

FERSEN. What's that.

MARIE. *(covers mouth, giggling)* One of Louis' watch springs //

FERSEN. No!

MARIE. YES!

(laughter)

MARIE. I hid it. I forgot I had it, look it's all rusty //

FERSEN. Louis and his clocks.

MARIE. Yes.

> (pause)

FERSEN. *(sad smile)* He was wrong you know…

MARIE. About?

FERSEN. We should never have called the troops that day.

MARIE. Why not?

FERSEN. The assembly wanted equality, he could have given them that.

MARIE. So you believe in this?

> this…*democracy*?

FERSEN. Of course not. The surface equality of a single class of people makes the exercise of power that much easier;

> It's just a diversion.

MARIE. A diversion?

FERSEN. Power can't be shared that's not the nature of it.

MARIE. No it's like an ether…

FERSEN. No such thing as equality…

> (beat)

MARIE. Liberty…

FERSEN. *(nods no)* It's an illusion…

> [STOP]

MARIE. *(the question that's been haunting her)* Has has my life been a *diversion*?

> (pause)

FERSEN. Don't get eaten up by regrets

> Not now.

MARIE. Should I have married you? or gone away with you?

FERSEN. You couldn't.

MARIE. *(something primal and vulnerable)*

> But you *cared* for me.

(beat)

Maybe these kings and queens and frilly things aren't
for me.

(beat)

I don't know anymore.
It's like some awful dream
and it's never been mine.

FERSEN. What.

MARIE. My life.

FERSEN. Then wake up.

*(FERSEN transforms into the Executioner; over the
following he mimes tying MARIE's hands behind her
back, the ritual of execution; she's oblivious.)*

MARIE. *(faraway)* How will you see me a hundred years
from now?

FERSEN. A butterfly with opalescent wings.

MARIE. You're my only friend.

(MARIE is now on the guillotine plank.)

MARIE. Fersen. Do you know
I dreamed they pushed me on the guillotine plank
I did and I felt it
I felt my head tighten in the vise
I thought they'd crush it;

(small laugh)

And I had an itch behind my neck but couldn't scratch
it how dumb.

FERSEN/EXECUTIONER. It's not a dream it's real
Wake up to it.

MARIE. *(oblivious)* They hacked off my head
held it high to thunderous cheers
stuffed it between my dead legs
dumped my body on the grass somewhere
threw it in an unmarked grave…

(Drumroll, shouts.)

FERSEN/EXECUTIONER. Wake up.

MARIE. But then I became the stuff of history,
And they couldn't kill me

(She smiles sadly.)

And when I awoke I thought:
"I have come into life now
Forever."

*(The shouts get louder, more feral. The lights grow
blindingly bright. Snap to black. Silence.)*

End of Play

Marraige?

SOME THOUGHTS ON PRODUCTION

HAIR

In many ways this is a story about hair. In the premiere production of the play we were able to chart Marie's demise through the progressive diminution of hair. And the gigantism of the wigs (particularly in the first scene) added to the surrealism and wild theatricality of the production. At Soho Rep, however – for both economic and dramaturgical reasons – the wig changes in between scenes seemed to impede the play's whiplash speed – we opted for a single wig for Marie in each act. There were elements of both approaches I liked, and I suppose in my ideal world the two approaches could be combined (we would see the three foot wigs in the opening, but there would be maybe three or four wig changes over the course of the play as opposed to say, eight or nine). But in general, I would err on the side of efficacy. Don't get too caught up in the wigs if they start to hamstring the storytelling.

The haircut in Act Two proved to be far more of a logistical trial than I imagined when I wrote it into the play. Getting a haircut off a wig to look real was really hard. We discussed non-literal ways to address the haircut (could they mime the haircut? What if they were on opposite sides of the stage acting out a haircut?). But ultimately we felt that the scene was too physical, and that the violence and intimacy had to be immediate. So our wig designer, after much nerve-racking trial and error, designed a rather magical, special wig with strands of actual hair attached in clumps by rubber bands, and the actor playing the Revolutionary was rather convincingly made to appear as though he were cutting Marie's hair. There might be other ways to do this haircut, but FYI: this turned out to be a great solution to a seemingly impossible conundrum.

COSTUMES

At Yale and ART the costumes were rather lavish and there were many costume changes. For the Soho Rep production we found it was best to strip the iconology down so that each character has their one iconic costume. Marie's one outfit for the entire show was stripped from here midway through Act Two and was replaced by a worn and tattered shift. Both ways can work, but I do feel that the constant costume changes for Marie disrupt the whiplash disorientation she's meant to experience over the course of the play, so that's something to watch for.

SHEEP

The Sheep is enigmatic, and he should stay enigmatic in production. He belongs to the register of the uncanny, of dreams. One thing we realized early on was that the actor playing the sheep is really more of an animating principle (the soul, as it were) of the sheep. We decided to give him a bit of a shape-shifting presence – so that in the first scene the actor entered in mainly all white, animating a small sheep puppet. In his next appearance at L'Hameau, Marie was surrounded by stationary sheep puppets, and late in the scene, this actor "possessed" the identity one of these sheep. In the final appearance of the sheep at the Conciergerie, the actor appeared with no puppet, as he had now come to embody the spiritual essence of the Sheep. There are many ways to accomplish this without being literal (putting an actor in an actual sheep costume, etc) but that's one idea.

WOLF

Again, we were stymied by how to do the transformation from Sheep to Wolf so that it had the sense of nightmare, wasn't too literal, but was at the same time coherent and dramatically effective. For the ART production our puppet designer, Matt Acheson, created a brilliant shadow puppet for the Wolf. It was visually stunning, but when we started working with the shadow puppet we all found it too conceptual (and somewhat confusing that we were now suddenly in a play with shadow puppets). We tried it a bunch of ways, and in the end had Marie's embrace of the Sheep slowly, invisibly transform into a kind of suffocation – so that she's suddenly struggling and screaming and trying to break away from him. The horror of this moment was augmented by the sound design and it was truly terrifying – and stayed true to the nightmare logic of the play. I'm sure there are any number of ways to make this moment really effective; as long as it relies on the actual human terror and not gimmickry.

RIOT

In early production meetings my director voiced her worry that staging an actual 'riot' would be too literal (which she was right to do), and had a horror (again rightly), of people running around with blackened teeth and dirty clothes a la Les Miserables. She wanted to try something a little more expressionist and figurative. The solution we came up with for the Yale/ART production was to drop a sheet of 'dirt' (fashioned from dyed cork pieces) on the lead actress from the fly-space – a visceral, jolting moment that symbolized the crashing halt in Marie's world. We then kept the dirt on stage for Act Two – which beautifully represented the thematic divide in the script between culture and nature. The Soho Rep production took place in a 74-seat black box with no fly-space, so rather than try to recreate the same effect, we projected titles onto the stage and had the lead actress, Marin Ireland, read them as they appeared – so that Marie was reading about and responding to the events of her life. The riot was less visceral, but it was equally terrifying (Marie's dissociation as she read about her life was eerie) and we did it on a budget. There are a number of ways to approach the theatricality of this moment, but I do feel that veering away from the literal is for the best. (I've included the titles that we used at Soho Rep in this published version if you want to go that route.)

DOUBLING/CAST SIZE

There are different ways to execute the doubling, but the doubling I recommend is the one listed in the character breakdown. At Soho Rep we also had the actress playing Lamballe portray the Royalist, which worked well both thematically and theatrically. I like the idea that everyone except members of the Royal Family and the Sheep play different roles. The characters that may not double are Sheep, Marie (obviously), Louis, and the Dauphin.

Initially I broke down the casting so that different actors would play the different Revolutionaries. At both Yale/ART and Soho Rep, we decided to use one actor to play all three of those parts. Even though they are literally different people, it gives the character a totemic aspect, which I found worked very well.

At Yale/ART, going along with the literalization of the excess and decadence, we had a 'coterie' who functioned as servants, dressers, etc. While I can imagine an extremely lavish production with tons of servants, the play can be done extremely stripped down with no servants. Both work really well.

DAUPHIN

I feel strongly that a child actor should be used for this role (should not be played by an adult actor, a puppet, etc.)

ACCENTS

The play isn't a history play and it isn't contemporary; it exists in its own universe with its own idiom. Please don't use 'period' accents. Don't go out of your way to over-colloquialize the French, but don't feel the need to roll every (or any) R. By the same token, please don't make Marie a "Valley Girl." Whatever comments the play makes about "now" should be accidental.

STAGE DIRECTIONS

Please don't cross out stage directions in this play. I'm aware of the school of "let's just ignore the stage directions and make up our own!" And certainly, this play invites a certain directorial invention – and, in fact, demands it. Part of the fun of doing a production of this play is inventing the world of it. That said, please don't invent new scenographic elements or add new characters. I can see how it might be tempting to put Marie Antoinette in one of the Saw films and have Jacobins come at her with chainsaws instead of give her a haircut.

Please don't do that.

MARIE

The play, especially in the first half, is propelled by anxiety and panic. It is a mistake to play Marie as relaxed in these scenes – the tension has got to be there. The surface banality needs to be counterpointed with this underlying anxiety for the play to really work.

Marie's anxiety gets shunted into a sort of a wild hydroplaning speed. The play is scored to this effect. The speed is punctuated with abrupt shifts, frightening gaps and silences. The music of the play is deliberately jerky and unstable.

I've found that when one doesn't pay strict attention to the moment-to-moment shifts, to the volatile changes in the tone and character, the play becomes blurred and it trivializes the subject matter and characters. Don't look for linear, steady arcs – it's a bit more like an EKG.

Please be vigilant about not commenting on the character of Marie. The comedy, in particular, should come from the emotional truth of the character – not from telegraphing. It is sometimes tempting to want to play her as 'spoiled' or 'decadent' – particularly in the first half of the play. But this really does cheapen the character.

There are certain moments in the first act that anchor her deep pain and trauma – so that when the revolution comes, it is not just some random external element impinging, it is mirroring some instability that already lives in her. Please pay close attention to these moments – they pay dividends.